The Peppermint Man

A Novel

Matthew Alan Hughes

Hope you enjoy, thanks!

Dream Writer Press

Copyright © 2012 by Matthew Alan Hughes

All rights reserved. This book or any portion thereof may not be reproduced or used in any manner whatsoever without the express written permission of the publisher except for the use of brief quotations in a book review.

This is for you Shanda, you might not always understand me, but you always support me. I love you!

The

Peppermint Man

Prologue

The thing's laugh was like the sound of finger nails being drawn across a black board. It was a high-pitched scream that came from the pit of its gut, and made the boy's ears hurt. When the thing laughed it looked like an evil clown—like the one in that movie called "It" he had watched with his father one night, long ago—right down to the exaggerated size of its blood-red lips. Its head bobbed around loosely, as if no muscles or bones connected to it to the rest of its body. When the boy thought he could take no more of the laughter, it pressed one clinched fist into its mouth, and the mad laughter became an even more maddening giggle. Then it burped—a loud, gassy burp that stank even from across the room—and the happiness was replaced by a glare. An evil glare the boy had come to recognize. And fear.

They were in a room the boy recognized but couldn't quite remember—things had become strange since his imprisonment here had begun. The walls were damp concrete blocks covered in patches of green-black mold. A long work bench stood against one wall, with a rusted table saw bolted down on it. Rows of canned vegetables lined two wooden shelves mounted above the workbench; some of them had lost their airtight seals, their contents long since rotted away. The air reeked of mildew and something worse. Something darker and more animalistic.

The smell radiated from the thing that was holding him prisoner. It came out in the sweat that constantly seemed to drip from its brow and in every breath it took. It was the smell one might expect if to find in the den of a hibernating but very rabid bear that was waiting for some hiker to wander close enough to wake it from its slumber. But this bear wasn't slumbering any more. This particular bear had long since awakened.

It looked at Billy and smiled, and the boy frowned. He knew bears did not smile. In his head he sometimes thought of it as a bear, just like he sometimes thought of it as a clown. But he knew it was something else. Something that he knew very well, but that knowledge stayed locked somewhere just out of his grasp. He started to think about it, and then his thoughts were broken as the thing raised its eyes to the ceiling and screamed at the top of its lungs.

It was naked except for a pair of soiled boxer shorts.

(Bears do not wear boxer shorts!)

Its bare chest and arms were splattered with still drying blood. In one hand the thing held a rusted hatchet, and in the other, something else. His young mind thought it looked like an overgrown pineapple. He loved pineapple. He used to eat pineapple at the beach with his mother and father, but that was before the bear (clown) came. Now they never went to the beach. Now they never went anywhere. The bear was afraid to go outside while the sun was still shining. It said there were people out there that would hurt them.

But it went outside sometimes. It left by itself, but it never came back alone.

The bear started pounding the pineapple-thing against the workbench, and its juices splattered all over the two of them. After several minutes of thrashing, it turned the pineapple around and yelled into a pair of glazed over eyes. But that wasn't right, Billy knew. Pineapples didn't have eyes! As he stared at it, the pineapple suddenly became his mother's head. She seemed to be staring at him, so he smiled and waved. She didn't wave back because she was a pineapple, and pineapples didn't have arms. But how had his mother become a pineapple?

"Do you feel better now?" the bear yelled at the boy's mother. Then it screamed at the top of his lungs and launched her across the basement of their house. That's where they were, he realized as his mother (the pineapple) smashed against the far wall. They were in his parents' basement, where he had never been allowed to go. His daddy didn't want him down there with all of his power tools. That's why the bear came. It came because he'd broken the rules and gone into the basement. "I don't want no pie! How about you, Billy?"

The boy shook his head. He didn't feel like eating pie anymore, but even if he had, he was too scared of the thing to disagree. Bad things happened when someone disagreed with the bear. All he wanted to do was go upstairs and go to bed, but the bear wouldn't let him.

Their imprisonment started days or even weeks earlier; Billy really had no way of knowing which. Three times the bear had left and came back with little girls. They weren't here anymore. They had gotten sick after the bear touched them, and then it had used the hatchet to make them stop crying. It had worked; they never cried again. Once they were quiet, the bear had taken them home again.

Billy was sad, because he never got to play with any of their visiters. They hadn't been good, so the bear had touched them and they'd cried. The bear didn't like that. It didn't like people who cried. His daddy hadn't liked "cry-babies" either. He'd spanked Billy until he couldn't walk once because he'd been crying.

That was when he was still little. Now he was a big boy. He was almost four and slept in a big boy bed. And he'd learned not to cry, because only bad boys cried. He wished his daddy was here instead of the bear. He looked at the bear, trying to wish it away, and for a moment he though he saw his father's face.

Then the bear screamed at the top of its lungs again. It grabbed a dirty pair of jeans from the corner. When it had them on it reached into a bowl on the workbench, and pulled out a handful of peppermint candies. It shoveled several into its own mouth, then handed one to Billy. The boy thanked the thing as he ate the candy, but he had to hold back his tears. Peppermint made him think of his father, and how badly he wished he would come back.

Billy's father loved peppermint candies. He kept a bowl full of them on the desk in his study, and sometimes they would eat one piece after another as they played in the floor with the boy's Hotwheels.

"You be good, Billy," the bear said as a grin broke back across its face. "I have to go find you another friend."

Billy sat quietly on his stool as the bear stomped up the stairs. When it was out of sight, the boy got up and walked over to his mother. Her pineapple head lay next to her body, which the bear had left in the corner. He grabbed her by the hair and tried to make her head fit back onto her neck. But it didn't work right. Something was wrong with her. She'd been sick since the bear used the hatchet on her.

"Mommy?" he asked softly. "Do you need a doctor?"

She just stared at him. He lay her head gently down and turned to look around the basement. He wanted to go upstairs and sleep, but the bear wouldn't be happy with him. He might yell, and then Billy might cry. He didn't want to cry. He wanted to be a good boy.

He sat back down on his stool and drifted off to sleep. He dreamed of his father and mother, happily playing with him on the beach. Out on the water a tiny sail boat drifted by in the distance, and Billy wondered what it would be like to be out there, so far from shore.

The he heard the bear's footsteps coming down the stairs.

"I brought you another friend, Billy," the bear screamed. The thing had to yell to be heard over the screams

of the girl it was carrying. It clumped down the last few steps and tossed the small girl it was holding to the ground. Her head hit the concrete floor hard, and she screamed louder. "She's not being a good little girl though, Billy. There are a lot of bad little boys and girls out there. All the bad little kiddies cry. You don't cry like a bad little boy. You aren't a bad boy, are you Billy? See if you can make her be quiet. She's making my head hurt."

Billy ran to the girl as the bear went to the corner and lay down. Within seconds it was snoring, and the sound was like the growling of an angry animal. (A bear!) The girl was naked, but that wasn't unusual. The bear liked to touch its friends before bringing them back to the basement.

"Please, quit crying," Billy whispered to her. "He doesn't like it when you cry."

No matter what he said, she kept crying. He bit his lips and fought back his own tears. He didn't want the bear to take her away too. It was lonely here in the basement. But he didn't want to cry, because then he would be a bad boy too. Then he felt a hand close on his shoulder. The bear was back, and he looked angry. It held the hatchet out in front of itself and shook it at the naked little girl. It raised his head towards the ceiling and screamed angrily.

"She's making my head hurt, Billy," the bear growled. Then it held the hatchet out to the boy. "You make her be quiet. You've seen me do it, you know how. Make her stop crying or I'm going to get mad."

The thing turned and went back to its dirty corner to lie down, naked once again except for its dirty underwear. Billy looked at the hatchet and frowned. The girl continued to cry, and he knew what he had to do. He wanted to cry, but couldn't. If he didn't stop her, he would get in trouble. So he raised the hatchet...

#

"He woke up screaming again last night," Karen Jackson said as they watched Billy Jones playing with the other children on the playground. She was nervous. He was an incredibly sweet child, but he wasn't doing well. He still woke up in the middle of the night screaming his head off, and in arts and crafts he often drew some very disturbing pictures. The teachers were threatening to have him removed from the class, or even the school if he didn't stop drawing those images, but she wasn't even sure he knew what he was drawing. She was scared child services were going to take him away, and that would be devastating for a child who was already teetering on a very dangerous ledge. "He didn't remember the dream, but...but he was scared."

Dr. Van Miller nodded and jotted notes down in his pocket-sized notebook. He had been Billy Jones's caseworker since the boy entered the system, now almost five years in the past. He'd seen the boy go from a four-year-old that would scream until he fell into a disconnected coma-like state, to an eight-year-old who could almost function at a normal level. After everything the boy had been through, even that much progress was almost a miracle. In the beginning he hadn't even been sure the boy would ever see the outside of Stony Point Mental Health Facility. It had seemed for a while that Billy would never even be able to speak in complete sentences.

But after all that progress, he still wasn't sure what the future would bring. During the last two months there had been a setback. No one knew the cause it, but something had brought back the nightmares and the screaming. It could be anything from a smell to seeing someone who looked like his father or one of his victims. And until they knew what it was, there was nothing they could do except either let it be or lock the boy back up inside Stony Point. Dr. Miller really didn't want to put the boy back there, because that would surely be the end of his recovery. Taken away from a normal life, the boy's delicate mind could permanently disconnect.

"So he's still drawing those pictures?"

Karen Jackson nodded and started to cry. She passed two pieces of construction paper to Miller. In the shaky hand of a small child were two very disturbing drawings. One showed a woman with a bloody, pineapple shaped head. A naked man stood behind her holding a bloody hatchet in the air. In the second drawing the same man was sleeping atop a pile of bloody corpses. A small stick figure stood to one side and was now holding the hatchet.

"He doesn't even remember drawing them," she said.

"I wish I knew what was triggering this," Miller thought aloud. "But we don't know enough. When the stuff with his father happened, Billy couldn't tell us anything. His conscious mind had blocked it all out. A three-year-old has hard time remembering things anyway, even without going through as what he went through."

Billy was now pushing a swing for a smaller girl. You would never know by watching the children laugh and carry on that three of the six had come from extremely violent backgrounds. None of them were as violent as Billy's, but they were still bad. Susan Barnes had seen her mother rapped and stabbed to death by a mugger. Wes Clark had been through two horrible events. First, he'd been in the car with his mother when a guardrail had beheaded her. Then he'd been the one to find his father's body after he killed himself with a shotgun. But out there, all by themselves, they seemed just like the other children. Like they didn't have a care in the world except their friends and the playground around them.

"But he's a tough kid," the doctor told her. "We just have to help him take it slowly."

"How do you do that?"

Dr. Miller shook his head. There was really no good solution to the problem. It was something he would have to face one day, but could an eight-year-old deal with bringing that much horror back? He'd forgotten his murderous father and everything he'd been through. Could he handle bringing it all back? Miller didn't think so, at least not yet. They were still trying to help him get back to normal. When he got a little older, maybe then he could deal with what he'd forgotten.

"I guess we just keep going the way we are," Miller said as he folded the drawings and put them into his briefcase. "Maybe we can find out what's triggering these nightmares, and then we can do something productive. Otherwise I think we just have to wait it out. We let him heal himself."

That wasn't what Karen wanted to hear, and for that Dr. Miller was very sorry. He knew she wanted a quick solution, hell he wanted a quick solution. She wanted him to wave his magical wand and make the dreams go away. She wanted him to make Billy a whole child again. He wished it were that easy, but it wasn't. The human mind was a fragile thing, especially when it belonged to a young child. Sometimes the best solution was to let things happen on their own.

He had a lot of respect for the woman at his side. Karen took these trouble kids in because she wanted to help, even though it made her own life more difficult. The world could use more people who cared that much. As long as there were people like that he could believe there was hope for every one of these poor kids.

The children left the swings behind and headed for the slide, giggling all the way. It horrified Van Miller that people would put such innocent children through what these had been through. He didn't even want to imagine the things the children Billy's father killed had been through. He wasn't sure which one would be worse. As a physiologist he knew he should say death was worse, because the mind can be repaired. But in his heart he wasn't sure. Even if they helped the boy get over his early childhood memories, they would still be there just waiting for something to trigger them. No amount of counseling could rid him of that curse.

The Peppermint Man would be with him every day of his life. At least he could believe that those little girls had gone on to a better place where what Ralph Jones did wouldn't matter. A place where he was sure that Ralph Jones would never be allowed.

But what about Billy? Miller was supposed to believe that every mind could be healed, but he had his doubts. Ralph Jones had been beyond help. He too had had come from a troubled childhood. His father, a decorated war hero, had come back from Germany a changed man. He was an alcoholic, prone to beating his wife and children. And in the end he'd killed them all, except for Ralph, who had been at college when his father suffered the final break.

"The Peppermint Man," Karen said, shaking her head. "What kind of name is that for a serial killer? They're supposed to be called names like Jack the Ripper and the Boston Strangler…not 'The Peppermint Man'."

"Peppermint was his trademark," Miller reminded her, although she knew the story. "He ate it all the time, even before the killings we know of. He ate so much of it he left traces of it all over his victims. The boy's subconscious mind associates peppermint with his father, and all the bad things he did. That's why Billy can't eat it without getting sick."

Dr. Van Miller really didn't want to take the boy out of this environment. He strongly believed that Billy would benefit from interacting with healthy children and a loving mother and father figure. Some of his colleagues had different opinions, but so far the case had been left up to him to decide. Unless there was some unforeseen setback, he didn't see his opinion changing.

Part One

"Billy"

Chapter One

Eighteen Years Later
Miltonboro, Kentucky

The sun felt good on his bare arms. It was the first time he'd been out of the garage since six o'clock that morning, and he wanted to enjoy every second. Billy Jackson sat on the tailgate of his pickup and pulled out his lunch box. He ate the same thing every day—although he always thought about bringing something different. In the end, he didn't like change. As he opened the refrigerator he might be thinking of taking something different—a turkey sandwich or a Hot Pocket for example—but when he slammed the lid closed he would have two ham and cheese sandwiches and two sodas. The crusts would be trimmed off, and the mayonnaise would be in a separate container, not on the bread. Putting it on the bread in the morning left would leave the sandwiches soggy by lunch.

Phil's Auto Mart was a small car lot in a small town, but he loved working there. His coworkers were nice, and no one cared if he preferred to stay to himself. Although they asked him nearly every day to join them at O'Doul's for a beer after work, Billy always politely turned them down and they never seemed to care. Mostly they just gave him a car to work on and left him alone. Sometime in high school he'd discovered his natural mechanical ability. And so he'd gone off to vocational school and learned his trade. Then he'd moved halfway across the state, leaving the only family he'd ever known behind.

No one had approved of his choice of homes, but Billy was now an adult and free to live anywhere he pleased. Coming back to the town of his birth had been a big step for him, one which no one else had seemed to think he was ready to take. But he'd come back, and none of the old nightmares had returned. The problems that had kept him in and out of Stony Point for two decades finally seemed to be in the past. A deep, hidden part of him had been afraid of what he would find in Miltonboro. He'd been afraid that people would remember his name, and remember what had happened. He was afraid people would want him to pay for what had happened. But all he had found was a satisfying job and a happy life. And the girl of his dreams.

Billy looked up at the warm sun and smiled. This winter had been a bad one—a foot of snow had fallen twice from Thanksgiving to New Years—but the weather had broken and spring was well on the way. In the last week the average temperature had been sixty degrees. He'd stopped wearing jackets and started wearing short-sleeved shirts for the first time since September. He'd stopped eating lunch in the break room and started eating outside, because he liked the fresh air—and he was a little claustrophobic. Maybe he would even take up fishing.

Dr. Miller was very happy that he'd found a career that made him happy, which was good enough to make Billy happy. Although he'd never said it aloud, he loved his therapist. The man had helped him through a lot of hard times, and sometimes it felt like the doctor had gone through all of them with him. It was a bond he would never share with anyone else, even his stepparents. He loved the Jacksons, but it was Miller that he wanted to make proud, not them. In a weird sort of way, Dr. Miller was like a father to him.

Billy had had some bad experiences before leaving Louisville. When he started vocational school, he'd received threatening letters in the mail. At first he had been able to shake it off, but they kept coming. He'd started to fear for his own safety, and then the safety of his friends. Then the panic attacks had started and the dreams had come back. He'd been hospitalized for a week, and institutionalized for a month. That was when he'd known that he had to leave Louisville. Somehow his secret had found him out, and he would never be able to live a normal life with people always accusing him. He needed a fresh start, somewhere they wouldn't expect to find him.

He'd never figured out who exactly *they* were. It had begun with a simple typed note that said "We know who you are and what you did." When it had been that simple it hadn't seemed all that important. When photographs from the crime scene had started accompanying the notes, a feeling of dread had settled over him. The final straw had been a series of letters threatening him, his stepparents, his roommates and even his dog—a Yorkie named Snot that had never hurt anyone in its short but happy little life. Out of concern for their own safety, his roommates had asked him to leave.

So he'd found a job over the Internet, and moved everything he owned across the state. That had brought him to the first place he'd ever been happy. Although Dr. Miller and his stepparents were concerned for his mental health, for the first time in his life he felt free.

Billy Jackson finished his lunch and put the trash back in his cooler. He stashed the lunchbox in the passenger's side floorboard of his truck and headed back towards the garage. He had an oil change on a Monte Carlo waiting for him, and then there was a Chevy Blazer with a faulty computer core. He woke up every morning looking forward to his work, because he could get into it and the day would fly by. Then he could clock out, pick up a movie and head home to relax.

"Good job on that GT this morning," his boss said as he walked into the garage. Mr. Butler was a pleasant man with a portly belly that always made Billy think about Santa Claus. "Don't get many like that one around here."

Billy whistled. "No sir, it sure was a beauty," he said. "I'd sure like to get my hands on one of those."

Phil Butler smiled. "Yeah, wouldn't we all?" he said with a laugh. He fished a handful of peppermint candies out of his pocket and offered them to Billy. The boy cringed.

"Oh, no thank you sir," he said, his stomach suddenly feeling like it needed to empty his lunch. He bit his lip and fought off the memory that tried to come flying back. "I can't eat peppermint, sir. Upsets my stomach."

"Keep up the good work, Jackson," Mr. Butler said as he shoved a peppermint into his mouth. Billy stared after his boss for a moment as he wondered deeper into the shop.

The afternoon flew by, as always. By five he was starting his truck and ready to head for home. He waved to some of his coworkers who were milling around, trying to decide whether or not to go for an afternoon beer at Murray's Bar-they had the same discussion everyday, before deciding beer was a good idea-and headed out of the parking lot. The first few months he'd been in town they had asked him to join them just about every afternoon, but he'd declined enough, they'd mostly stopped asking. As much as he would have liked to make new friends, he feared getting close to anyone. Miltonboro was not a big place; there were surely some folks around who would still remember Ralph Jones and his boy. From the few old photos he'd seen of his old man, there was a definite resemblance. If he got close to anyone they might discover who was.

It took five minutes to get from work to the video store, and then another five to get to his apartment building. He sang along with the radio as he drove, only stopping when he came up on someone who might see him singing and laugh. By the time he got to his apartment he was in a pretty good mood, as he usually was these days.

#

Billy had never lived on his own, so the move across Kentucky had scared him. Growing up he'd lived in a household constantly inhabited by four or five foster children, and after vocational school he'd moved in with two of his friends from high school. As far as he had been concerned, it was the best setup a twenty-something could hope for. You got to split the bills three ways, and your best friends were right down the hall.

Billy had moved into a loft apartment with Douglass Mills and Otis Norris, his best friends in high school, and the four months they'd lived there had been the best of his life. They threw parties for their other friends, and went to every U of L home game.

But things at the apartment had gone bad when the letters started coming. His friends were familiar with his past, but they assumed it was in the past. When people started sending threatening letters, they'd quickly changed their minds. His friends wanted nothing but the best for him, but neither boy was willing to sacrifice his own safety. One night they'd called him to the living room and broke the news.

"We want you to move out," Douglass had said.

"Move out?" Billy had laughed, thinking they were joking. "I don't have anywhere to go."

"You've been getting all of these threatening letters, Billy," Otis Norris added. "We…we just don't feel safe with you living here."

They hadn't felt safe, Billy thought. A year later and half a state away, he shook his head. It hadn't really bothered him that they wanted him to leave, especially once he'd discovered they feared for their own safety. Their safety had been the thing that ultimately convinced him to move. He was worried more about his friends more than himself.

#

If he hadn't met Sarah, he wasn't sure how he would have ended up. People had always told him that love could happen anywhere at anytime, but being the pessimist that he was, he hadn't believed it. Then one day he'd been out for a walk and literally ran into her. He was doing laps around the apartment complex that he called home, entirely lost in his own thoughts, when he rounded a corner and collided with someone.

Sarah was a small girl—only five foot tall—but the first time he saw her she'd scared him. As she picked herself up of the ground she glared at him as if she were about to rip his head off. Then she saw how embarrassed he seemed, and her expression had softened. That night had ended with a trip to a coffee shop across town. Within a week they were dating, and by the end of their second month together she had started spending every night at his place.

She was there most nights when he got home from work, welcoming him with a warm hug and a kiss. For just a moment all of the worries of his life seemed to fade away.

While the embrace lasted, she was the only thought on his mind.

"How was your day?" she asked after letting him go.

"It was great," he told her, which was the truth. In the all the time he'd worked at the garage, he'd never had a real bad day. Some were better than others, but all of them were pretty good. "I got to work on a GT in mint condition."

"That's good," Sarah said, before heading back towards the kitchen. "Some mail came for you this afternoon. It's on the coffee table."

Billy laid his lunchbox down on the couch and picked up the simple white envelope that was lying on the coffee table. He turned it over in his hand and frowned. There was no postage and no return address on the front of the envelope, just his name printed in big block letters.

"Did someone bring this by the apartment?" he called into the other room.

"No, it was in the mailbox."

"It doesn't have any postage."

"Well it was in there," she said.

He sat down on the couch next to his lunchbox and fished his pocket knife out of his jeans. He clicked the lock blade open and slid it across the top of the envelope, slicing the paper open. Two items fell out into his lap; a small white postcard and an aged photograph. He turned the latter over and his heart skipped a beat.

A young girl with silky blond hair stared back at him from far back in his past. She was thirteen when the picture had been taken, he knew, because he'd seen this photo before. In fact it had been taken on her thirteenth birthday. She wore a cheesy party hat, and held a birthday cake out in front of her, showing off the Dukes of Hazard logo that had been skillfully crafted out of icing. She was smiling beautifully, not a care in the world.

"Oh God," Billy muttered.

"Did you say something, hon?" Sarah asked from the other room. He didn't answer, because he was somewhere else.

Her name was Glenda Baker, and she was his father's seventh victim. He'd grabbed her one afternoon as she walked home from a little league baseball game, and the authorities didn't find the body for four months. She had vanished only two days after the photo in his hands had been taken. Miltonboro had been in a panic after the first six victims, but the disappearance of Glenda Baker had pushed the town over the edge. So many parents pulled their children out of school that the schools had to close. The streets were disserted. Even at four Billy had understood that something bad was going on.

Billy could feel the panic attack building up. He had gotten used to the feeling when he lived in Louisville when this sort of thing happened every day, but he hadn't felt it since moving. Now it was back, and just as bad as ever. His heart raced, and a sharp stabbing feeling started somewhere behind his left eye. His throat threatened to close up, cutting off his breathing. He tried to lay the photograph aside, but his hand was shaking so bad that he just dropped it. It tumbled to the floor, Glenda Baker's smile taunting him.

"Not again," Billy whispered.

"You okay, hon?" Sarah asked, and suddenly she appeared. She was wearing the apron she always wore when doing dishes. Soapy water dripped from her upheld hands, to the brown carpet of their living room. She took one look at him and went pale. "Billy, are you okay?"

He couldn't answer. All he could do was stare at the photograph, which lay between his feet.

"Billy, tell me what's wrong," she demanded.

He had never told her about his father, because he'd been afraid of how she would react. Some people were uncomfortable just speaking with the offspring of a notorious serial killer. She was much more involved than that. *She's gonna leave me,* he thought, which made everything seem even worse. *She's going to find out about me and leave me!*

"Billy!" she nearly screamed. Then she was shaking him. For a moment his head cleared, and he saw how worried she was. "Billy, what's wrong?"

"In the medicine cabinet..." he said, barely able to get enough breath to speak. "In the medicine cabinet there's a pill bottle from my doctor. Get...get my pills."

Chapter Two

He was small again, trapped in the basement of his childhood home. The bear—he now knew it was his father, but in the dream he couldn't help but think of the monster as anything but "the bear"—was gone, but it would be back soon. It always came back. Even when he knew he was dreaming, he was afraid of what it would do when it came back.

Billy JAckson tried to take control of his dream, but he could never control them. When they had somewhere to take him, he was as trapped as a passenger on a Boeing 747. He was along for the ride, for good or bad. Normally when he dreamed it was the latter. His waking mind had come to terms with what his father had done, but his subconscious would not. The part of his mind that slumbered while he was awake didn't know that twenty years had come and gone. It thought the bear was still out there, waiting to get him.

Then he heard the sound of footsteps outside the house. Billy willed himself to scream for help, but no sound would come. The stomping footsteps proceeded across the kitchen, and then the basement door crashed open, thumping hard against inside wall, sending chunks of drywall flying.

For a moment he had hope that the police had come to rescue him. This time they would show up early and save him! Then one bare foot, followed by another appeared. After that the rail thin, blood smeared body that once belonged to his loving father appeared, a much smaller body clutched in his arms. The girl was nearly naked and trying to scream, but he'd shoved a knotted piece of cloth in her mouth.

"She's been a bad little girl, Billy," the bear said reproachfully. "A very very bad little girl."

Billy tried to move away, but he couldn't. His body refused to move from its perch atop one of the workbench stools. The bear crossed the room and threw the girl at his feet. Glenda Baker stared up at him, her eyes filled with tears.

"Only bad little boys and girls cry, Billy," the bear said. "I—" He stopped at the workbench and greedily snatched up a handful of peppermints. He shoved one into hiss twisted and blood smeared mouth. The next sound he made sounded to Billy's adult mind like an orgasm, but as a small child he hadn't had the words to describe it. "I think you know what we have to do to the bad little girls and boys!"

#

And then Billy was awake. The desire to scream at the top of his lungs filled him, and instead of waking Sarah he covered his face with a pillow. The scream escaped as little more than a stifled grunt. When the feeling had passed, he put the pillow back beneath his head and stared at the ceiling.

His vision swam as the medication continued to work on him. Every shadow in the room seemed to be exaggerated. The part of his mind that controlled his dream insisted that the bear could be out there hiding. Maybe he was behind the coat rack! Or the dresser.

He did not think that he would sleep again.

#

His alarm clock woke him just in time to take a shower and head to work. Billy had taken the pills plenty of time before, and they'd never put him out for more than three or four hours at a stretch. This time he'd been out for twelve. He still felt drugged when he pulled into his parking lot at the Phil's Auto Mart, despite a cold shower and a mug of coffee. He rested his forehead against the steering wheel and blinked, trying to clear his head. Not only was his head still foggy, now his head was beginning to throb. It was a dull pounding feeling deep in his temples.

At last he gave up and headed into the building. Everything had a surreal quality. It was like walking around in a waking dream. The lights seemed too bright, while everything in the room seemed too dark. The other mechanics were there like normal, but somehow they didn't seem to be real. They were like ghosts. His boss appeared in his office doorway and beckoned Billy over. He had the absurd idea that he could walk up to Mr. Butler and put his hand through the man's chest as if he were no more solid than a cloud of smoke.

"Morning, Mr. Butler," he said.

"You look rough, Bill," the man said. "Rough night?"

Billy nodded. "Yeah, I'm not feeling too well," he admitted. "I'll make it though. Just need to be up and walking around."

Mr. Butler nodded, but looked concerned. After a brief pause he headed back into his office.

Billy walked across the garage to the supervisor's desk, where a row of file separators was arranged. A name was tapped on each separator. He had to search to find his, because he couldn't seem to remember where it was. There were two folders in his tray. He flipped through them, barely able to read them because the letters kept trying to rearrange themselves. It looked like he had another oil change and a brake job scheduled.

By lunch his head was beginning to clear, and Billy was beginning to think he would make it through the day. He sat on the back of his truck and stared at his feet, wondering what was wrong with his medication. He would have to talk to a doctor about it. His stomach was growling, but there wasn't much he could do. He'd forgotten to pack lunch. He sipped on a soda he'd bought from the drink machine.

That was when the man who'd gotten the oil change came back. He was a short, fat man with a swollen red face, and a very angry expression. He stomped up to Billy's truck and demanded to speak with the manager. Billy pointed him in the right direction and went back to staring at his feet. A moment after the man vanished through the garage's bay doors, Mr. Butler started yelling.

"Billy, get in here!"

The young mechanic slammed his tailgate and stumbled his way into the building. Phil Butler, the oil change guy and the shop supervisor-Emmit Dixon-were standing just outside the boss's office glaring at him. Billy asked them softly what the problem was. Dixon started to get smart, but Phil put a hand on his shoulder. The man cursed and turned his back on them, but stayed within earshot.

"What did you do to this guy's car?" Phil Butler asked.

"I changed his oil."

"I know that was what you were supposed to do," the boss snapped. "But did you forget something?" Billy shook his head. "Well it would seem that you did. His car got a block away and the engine seized up. Wasn't a drop of oil in it."

"That's crazy; I put oil back in it."

"Then why don't it have any oil in it?" the car owner blurted. Billy looked from Phil to the man, not understanding. "Can you tell me that, boy? You just ruined my new car. I knew I shouldn't have brought it here! Should have gone to the dealer over in Pine Grove."

"But I put oil in it," Billy insisted.

"Well, we'll see about that," Dixon snapped and hurried across the garage.

"Billy, you've been here a long time and this just ain't like you," Phil said. "If you've got some problem, you don't need to be here. I'd rather you stay at home in bed than come in and screw something up like this. Do you have any idea how much it'll cost me to buy a new motor?" Billy nodded.

Emmit Dixon came running back across the garage, carrying something in his hand. He leaned over to Phil Butler and whispered something in his ear. The two men shared a glance, and then turned to him.

"You say you put the oil back in?" Dixon said. Before Billy could argue, he produced the plug from an oil tank. He held it up to him as if proving his mistake. "Then tell me, what is this?"

"Bill, I don't know what's going on with you today, but we can't have this kinda thing," Mr. Butler said. He was being very careful to control his words. Billy could see the anger beginning to boil behind his eyes. "Get your stuff and go home. I'll call you later this week and we can decide what to do. Maybe you just need some time off."

"But I-"

"I told you he screwed it up," the car owner blurted.

"Sir, I did it the way I was supposed to!" he insisted.

"I don't know what to think, Bill," Butler said. He took Billy by the arm and led him out of the garage's front bay doors. "I've got an angry customer, and a car I'm gonna have to buy a new motor for. I don't have time right now to figure out what happened. You just take a few days off, and hopefully things will be okay. Okay?"

"You can't honestly believe I left the oil drain plug out!" Billy yelled. "That's the first thing you learn in vocational school. I can't believe you think I'd be stupid enough to do that."

"I said I don't have time right now, Bill," his boss said angrily. "Get out of my sight right before I get mad. I have to take care of replacing this guys motor, thanks to you."

#

The local radio station had broken from format to cover a breaking news story. He was about to change the station, but what they were talking about caught his attention. Local authorities were conducting a countywide search for a missing girl. The announcer said the girl had who'd disappeared the previous night after being seen with a stranger. They asked that everyone who'd seen anything out of the ordinary between Savage Drive and Tradewater Road to call the police station immediately. The FBI was offering $50,000 to anyone with clues that would lead to the girl's return.

He shook his head and turned the radio up. Miltonboro was a place where he'd always felt safe, no matter where he was or what he was doing. Things like this weren't supposed to happen here, at least not any more. Los Angeles was one thing, but a rural Kentucky town was different. Children were supposed to be safe when they were out playing alone. This was a place where everyone knows your name. People didn't always lock their doors at night. Your neighbors were supposed be looking out for you. Old men gathered daily to play chess in the city park, whether it was sunny and warm or cold and dreary. It was the place where you expected at any moment to see a man in a sheriff's uniform and a barefoot boy with red hair whistling as they headed down the street towards the fishing hole. But in one night this little Mayberry had been transformed into a place as dark and scary as Los Angeles or New York. Once trusting neighbors would look at each other suspiciously. Parents would no longer let their children out of the house alone. It was happening all over again.

"We've got a missing twelve year old girl," Police Chief Wallace Williams said over the radio. "We believe that she was taken against her will, and we believe her to be in grave danger. Lacy Bennett was last seen near the Breeze Freeze at about eight o'clock last night. An eyewitness believes they saw her struggling with a man near the corner of Savage and Booth fifteen minutes later, which would have been about right if she were walking home from the ice cream shop. When our eyewitness circled back, there was no sign of the girl or the man.

"He is described as late 20s or early 30s, with short black hair. At the time he was seen the man was wearing a denim jacket and blue jeans. Lacy had on jeans and a blue hooded sweatshirt. She's five foot tall with blue eyes and straight blonde hair. If you saw anyone fitting these descriptions in that area last night, please contact us immediately. We want a happy resolution to this situation."

"I believe the father of Lacy Bennett is going to be...yes, he's getting ready to go live at a press conference in downtown Miltonboro," the DJ broke in. Then there was a brief pause, followed by a burst of feedback. A man cleared his throat.

"Lacy, I love you," the father began. "If you can hear me, I just want you to know that I love you. And your mother and your brothers love you. We're doing everything we can to get you home safely. Whoever you are...the one that took her...please bring her back to us. We need out daughter back. She means more to us than anything." The man began to sob uncontrollably, but they kept him on the air. "She's just a sweet, innocent little girl. There's no need to hurt her, or to hurt any of us. Please let her go. You can just drop her off at a bank, or a restaurant for all I car, but please let her go. We can't go on without her...she's our everything."

Billy's heart went out to the father on the other end of the radio. He knew the odds; he'd read them over and over again in the days before they had declared him mentally healthy. He'd needed to see proof that his father hadn't been the only crazy man out there. The odds of recovering a child that age after she'd been abducted weren't good. It was unreal that something like this could happen in a small town like Miltonboro. Only four thousand people called the small town home.

It was a heartbreaking story, and one that Billy could identify with, at least a little. His own father had abducted and killed eleven girls during a two-week period, and that was only the ones the authorities knew about. In the year leading up to his breakdown and finally his capture, over a hundred girls had gone missing in the area he hunted. Each one of them had left a family somewhere whose hope of a rescue had not turned out well. He wondered exactly how many fathers his own dad had put in this situation.

"Please, if you have any heart at all, bring my little girl home," the father went on. "Any harm you inflict on her, you're inflicting on all of us too." Then the man broke down into tears, and a second voice came on the radio. It was the sheriff again.

"I want to make a promise to whoever took this poor girl," the man said. "We will catch up with you. For your sake you had better hope Lacy is still okay, or you will pay. Miltonboro is not a town where you can do something like this and not expect to get caught. Someone will see you and recognize you, or you'll slip up. Your best option is to come forward now…"

Billy shut the radio off, unable to go on listening. The story was too close to home for him, in more than one way. His apartment complex was at the opposite end of Savage Drive from the Breeze Freeze. He drove by the little ice cream shop at least twice a day, and had never paid it any attention. Now every time he drove passed there he would think of his father, something that he hated to do. He would have to find a different path to work, if he were to keep his sanity.

That is if you still have a place to work, he thought sorely. He couldn't believe that he'd left the drain plug out of a car. He'd performed hundreds of oil changes in his lifetime, and he'd never once forgotten to put the plug back in. Billy ran through the events of that morning again and again, and even though they were clouded by the pills he'd taken the night before, he still remembered putting the drain plug back in.

He knew there had to be a rational explanation, but he couldn't come up with one. There was no question that the drain plug was left out, but how then had it happened? Billy shook his head as he drove. He'd never figure it out, he knew. Even if he had left the plug out, his mind would continue to insist that he'd put it back, because he'd always put it back. But he couldn't help but worry because of the drug induced haze he'd worked through all morning. What if he *had* left the drain plug out?

As he sat at a stoplight, he realized that he had nothing to do. His job was the only thing he really had, and now it was the middle of the day and he couldn't go there. And Sarah would still be at her job. To make matters worse, as the drug haze cleared, he was starting to get a headache. It was a dull pain behind his temples.

His thoughts drifted back to the envelope he'd gotten last night. Was it a coincidence that someone found out who he was one the same night that a girl was abducted?

Chapter Three

Billy Jackson pressed a hand to his forehead, trying to will the pain away. But it wasn't going. As a matter of fact it seemed to be getting worse. It had moved from his temples until it seemed to be concentrated in the backs of his eyes. It felt as if someone had pressed nettles into his pupils. His heart was racing too, as if he'd just finished running a marathon, and his chest was beginning to hurt. He thought he was having a heart attack. Everyone in the restaurant kept looking at him but he didn't care. He felt horrible. Sweat was starting to drip off of his forehead, but he was freezing.

"More coffee, hon?" the waitress asked.

He shook his head and asked her to bring the check. All the years he'd spent in counseling had resulted in him ending up like this. It was absurd. He thought he'd come to terms with his father, the monster, when he was still in high school. But every time he thought the nightmare was over, something or someone would cause send him back to where he'd been before. He understood that none of the things that had happened in the basement of his childhood home had been his fault, but on some subconscious level the guilt was still there. He couldn't get passed it. No matter how many counseling session he sat through, the past was still lurking in the back of his mind to jump out and grab him.

Billy was desperate for something that would calm his nerves, but he was afraid of his medication. What it had done to him last night wasn't what it was supposed to do. It was supposed to help him sleep, not get him high. He needed his head clear, especially if he was in danger of losing his job. But as he was now, his head wasn't going to be clear with or without the drugs. The way he was now he was probably going to end up hospitalized again. Then they would find out who he was and what he'd done. His life in Miltonboro would be over. People would protest and shout obscenities. Then they would start throwing objects at him, while continuing to protest and shout obscenities. He closed his eyes and wanted to cry.

Make her stop crying or I'm going to get mad.

Billy Jackson felt just as he had the last time he'd had a panic attack.

He was afraid that the people who had harassed him in Lousiville might find him again, or that a new group would start doing the same thing here. And if there were people evil enough to send him threatening letters, they might move on to more. They might break into his house when he was asleep and punish him for his deeds. Now he knew he couldn't take his medicine no matter what. He had to be awake and alert when they came, because they would come. They would come, and they would kill him. He peered nervously around the restaurant, wondering if they were watching him already.

Every shadow seemed to hold a threatening figure that was about to leap out and attack him.

Billy jumped up from his chair, nearly knocking over the waitress who was returning with his ticket. He absently apologized and pulled a wad of money from his pocket. He pulled out a few bills without even looking at them. He handed the money over and bolted for the door. He had to get away, just in case they were watching and waiting for him to let his guard down. The confused waitress stared after him, holding three twenty-dollar bills in her hand.

You aren't a bad boy, are you Billy?

He wondered if someone here had found him out, or if someone had followed him all the way from Louisville. The ones there had been dangerous; he'd known that then, although Dr. Miller had assured him it was just kids playing a stupid prank. It wasn't kids. It was the parents of one or all of the little girls his dad had abducted, and they were mad because they'd never gotten their revenge. They wanted to get their revenge of the son of the Peppermint Man, since they couldn't get the man themselves. He thought it must be them that followed him, because those people would never give up.

The sun was bright when he stepped outside. It hurt Billy's throbbing head, but somehow it seemed to make him feel better. He was glad to be out in the open, out where they couldn't get him without giving themselves away. But eventually the sun would go down, and when that happened he would need to protect himself. He needed to go home and find a weapon. Then he could get to a place where he would be safe.

A woman with a baby stroller rolled past Billy, heading for the restaurant. They baby inside was screaming its head off, wanting someone to pick it up. He covered his ears and wanted to scream. The baby was so loud. He wished its mother would pick it up and rock it so it would shut up.

Make her stop crying or I'm going to get mad!

Then the woman and her child disappeared through the front doors, which cut the screaming off. He wondered if that woman was in on this. Maybe she'd made her baby cry so it could drive him crazy. He wouldn't do it; he wouldn't allow them to drive him crazy. That was exactly what they wanted to do. They wanted him crazy so that when they killed him they would have an excuse. Who could blame them for killing a crazy man?

Billy shook his head. He knew he wasn't making sense. He knew there was no one out there trying to kill him or drive him crazy, but at the same time he believed everything. He clutched his head in both hands and stifled a scream. He knew he needed to be medicated, but he couldn't. He needed something to calm his nerves, without putting him to sleep, but anything he took would leave him unable to protect himself if they really were after him. He wished that he were back in Lousiville, so he could go see Dr. Van Miller. Doc could help him. He always helped.

He dug change out of his pocket and headed for a phone booth in the corner of the lot. He could always call Doctor Miller. He dropped the coins in and punched in the long distant number. His hands shook as he listened to the ringing. It seemed to be forever before the doctor answered the phone, and when he did he seemed unbelievably distant. Could he really help if he was so far away? Suddenly Billy didn't know if calling was a good idea. Maybe Miller would have him locked up.

"Hello?" the doctor asked impatiently.

"Doc?" he said softly.

"Billy, is that you?"

"Yeah, its me," Billy replied.

"What wrong Billy?"

He stared at the phone, wondering what he should say. He also wondered if the people trying to kill him had the phone booth tapped. Maybe they would hear everything he said, and then try to kill Miller. Billy wouldn't put it passed them. They were evil. When people focused so totally on revenge, it drove them to do things like that. Its what he would have done if he had been like them. On the other end of the phone Miller was asking him question after question, his voice beginning to sound very concerned.

"I've got a problems, Doc," he said at last. "They're after me again."

"What happened, Billy?" Miller asked.

"I...I got a photograph in the mail yesterday" Billy said sharply. "Just like before."

"Have you told anyone about your past?"

"No, not even Sarah," the boy said. "But they've found me again. They've found me and now they're doing it all again."

"Call the police, Billy," Dr. Van Miller told him. "Call the police and tell them everything."

"No!" Billy yelled before he realized he was answering a voice from far back in his memory. He slammed a fist angrily against his forehead.

"No what, Billy?"

Billy realized that no one was left on his side. They, whoever they were, had gotten to Doctor Miller and turned him. His old friend wanted him to get killed. He cursed under his breath and slammed the phone down. A child walking passed the phone booth turned to look curiously at him, and he gave her the finger. Her face swelled up, and then she started crying. She covered her face with dirty little hands.

All the bad little kiddies cry.

He glared at the girl, wanting to make her stop pouting. She didn't see, she was still covering his face and crying. Part of him felt bad for making the child cry, but another part of him was getting angry. Billy looked around, trying to decide what to do. Soon the girl's screaming would attract attention, and someone would come to find out what had happened. What if they thought he'd tried to hurt the little girl?

She's making my head hurt, Billy. You make her be quiet.

"Shut up," Billy muttered, whether he said it to the voice or the child he wasn't sure. He clinched his eyes closed and fought off a scream.

Only the bad kiddies cry, Billy.

Billy headed for his truck, deciding to avoid the situation altogether. As he pulled out onto the road, leaving the bawling child behind, he switched the radio on. Once again breaking news had broken into the music sweep.

"-we found the body of Lacy Bennett," the sheriff was saying. He sounded very tired and shaken. "We were conducting a search of the western side of town, when one of out volunteers found the body. At this time we have made positive identification."

"Can you tell us what happened?" a reporter asked.

"No, we're not taking any questions at the point, and there are a lot of aspects of this case we need to keep secret at the moment. All we can say is that this poor little girl was viciously murdered at some point last night. We still have no suspects in custody, so we want to ask everyone to please keep their children off the street. We don't know the full situation behind this murder, so we have to believe that it's not safe on the streets right now.

"The Sheriff's Department and the Miltonboro police department are using all available assets to track down this killer. We assure you that the monster that did this will pay. Our hearts and prayers go out to the Bennett family in their time of need. Once again we beg you, if you have any information in this case, please call the authorities and help us bring this killer to justice."

#

Billy paused just inside the door of his apartment. Had someone been here? He carefully surveyed the room and shook his head. What was wrong with him? He was being silly. There was no one after him. No one was trying to kill him. But he couldn't make himself believe it. He slammed the front door and stomped into his house, wondering what was going on.

His answering machine was flashing a dozen messages. Billy punched the delete button without listening to them. He was in no mood to listen to concerned messages from Doc Miller and his foster parents, especially with his paranoia telling him that the concern was false. As he sank into his recliner, the absurdity of that idea finally occurred to him. It wasn't like suddenly stumbling upon the meaning of life while hoeing the garden; it was more like looking back on something you'd said in a heated argument and realizing how stupid you sounded.

He remembered the breakdown he'd had in Louisville, the one that had finally sent him running all the way to Miltonboro. It had started like this, but that time it had taken a lot longer. The pictures and news clippings had been coming in the mail for weeks before he'd started feeling like this. His waking mind had been filled with conflicting ideas, each of which could randomly solidify themselves into facts. The process had ended with a month long stay in the hospital, under the constant monitoring of doctors and nurses. Dr. Miller had been by his side the entire time, assuring him that he was going to be okay.

He suddenly felt bad for hanging up on Doc. Van Miller had been nothing but good to him through all of the rough years. He'd been there when Billy had finally come face-to-face with the nightmare hidden in his subconscious, and he'd helped him deal with it. There weren't a lot of men who would be willing to do that. There were even fewer men who would be willing to do that and still be there to talk about the day-to-day problems. He'd also helped Billy recover from his breakdown, even though he was technically a child physiologist.

Billy's headache had finally begun to subside, and he hoped it would take the paranoia with it. He rubbed absently at his temple and tried to get the day straight in his mind. Tomorrow he would have to try to get things fixed at work, if he was going to keep working at Phil's. He still couldn't believe he'd left the drain plug out of the oil pan, but that was beside the point. Phil Butler and Emmit Dixon believed he'd done so, and there was really no chance of changing their minds. Short of paying for a new engine-which he couldn't afford-he wasn't sure what to do. He'd start by dropping by the garage to talk with his boss.

He also needed to call Dr. Miller and apologize. The man was no doubt pacing his office, trying to figure out how to contact him. Doc had been to good a friend to do this to him. He needed to know that Billy was really okay.

Cautiously he got up from the chair and headed for the phone, afraid the headache would come rushing back to him, but when it hadn't returned after two steps, he went the rest of the way across the room with ease. Maybe he was getting better. Maybe his near breakdown was just something brought on by the medication. At least he could hope and pray.

Billy lifted the receiver and dialed Miller's number. There was a pause, followed by the ringing of a phone on the far end of the country. It was getting late in Kentucky, but California was still two hours behind him. Doc's office should still be open. But the phone continued to ring and ring. After an eternity there was a click on the other end.

"You've reached the Office of Doctor Van Miller," Doc's voice said from the answering machine. "I'm sorry but we are currently out of the office. If you are a patient, please use my pager number; otherwise, leave your name and a message after the beep and we'll get back to you."

When the machine beeped he said, "Doc, this is Billy, I just wanted to let you know that I'm okay now. I was just having a rough day. Give me a call when you can, and, uh...I'm sorry about earlier."

Billy lay the phone down and looked around the room, trying to figure out what to do next. He wished Sarah was home, so he could tell her everything that was going wrong. As much as he wanted to keep his secret, she of all people had the right to know that he was the son of the Peppermint Man.

#

Billy was still sitting on the couch when Sarah came home from work. The tremors and the headache had finally stopped, and for the moment he felt okay. He didn't feel great, because in his condition he was like an acrobat teetering on a high wire raised above the center ring of a crazy circus. The least little thing could push him off of that wire, and the worst part was that he knew it and couldn't stop it.

Sarah took one look at him and knew something was wrong. The two of them had only been together for four months, but that was long enough for her to learn his moods. He hadn't had an anxiety attack since meeting her, but his moods often swung from extreme happiness to the opposite end of the spectrum. When he was like this, he felt like he was doing both at the same time.

"Oh baby, what's wrong?" she asked as she sat down next to him. She still wore her nurse's scrubs, and smelt like a hospital. "I know it must be something really private, but you've got to talk about it."

"I don't know how," he said, looking down at the photo on the table in front of him.

Sarah noticed what he was looking at and picked it up. For a moment he was embarrassed, because Glenda Baker and the others were his deepest darkest secret. And then he felt a rush of relief. He didn't have to keep it locked up inside anymore. He could tell her everything.

When Billy was finished talking, Sarah didn't say anything for a long time. He'd told her he would understand if she left him, but he desperately hoped that she wouldn't. In the few months that they'd been together, she had come to mean everything to him. He didn't want to imagine the hell his world would become if she left him.

"None of that is your fault, Billy," she told him at last. "Whatever…horrors you lived through, that was all your father's fault. Not yours. You can't go on blaming yourself for it."

"But I was there," he protested. "I could have done something."

"You were just a little kid," Sarah said forcefully.

He started to say something else, but she put her hand on his shoulder and pressed her lips to his. Just touching her could make everything new again. His father and everything he'd done was still there, but it was in the past. When they broke their embrace Billy started to cry.

All the bad little kiddies cry.

"Its okay, baby," she said, pulling him tighter. "You should have told me about all of this a long time ago."

"I know," he said through a sob.

"Let's go to bed," she whispered, and they did.

After they made love, he dreamed again.

Chapter Four

Billy woke the next morning, feeling surprisingly better. He also woke to the smell of bacon frying and coffee brewing. He crawled out of bed and stumbled into the kitchen, his mind still not quite in tune with his body. Sarah was at the stove, wearing one of his t-shirts. She smiled at him, and he smiled back, despite what he'd gone through lately.

"Shouldn't you be at work?" he asked as he wrap his arm around her waist and spun her around.

She pecked him on the cheek. "I'm sick today, can't you tell?" she said playfully. "I thought we could enjoy ourselves today. Maybe catch a movie or just go for a walk in the park."

"Sounds wonderful," he said with a smile, although in his mind he was worried about their finances. She still had to pay rent at her apartment, until the lease was up in a month and a half, and he had to pay his. But if he was without a job he wouldn't be able to.

"Hey stop that," she warned him when she was the look in his eyes. "Today we aren't worrying about anything or anybody else. We're just going to be together and have fun." She turned back to her cooking. "You under stand that, Mister?"

"Yeah, I understand," he replied. He wanted nothing more than to spend a day without worrying about anything, but he didn't know if he could do it. Worrying had always been a part of his life. He always had to worry about falling over the edge into the abyss that had controlled his childhood.

"What's playing today?"

"No clue."

"Well I can see that you're well prepared."

Sarah stuck her tongue out, and he laughed as he picked up the weekly paper that had come while he was still asleep. Nothing ever happened in Miltonboro, but he subscribed to the paper regardless. Just having it to read every Wednesday made him feel like he belonged. But when he opened the paper, he was greeted by a horrifying headline.

Second Girl Missing in Two Days.

"Oh good lord," he mumbled.

"What is it?" Sarah asked, not even looking up from the frying pan.

"Nothing," he lied, and started to read.

#

Sandy Moxley, 14, of Miltonboro left a friend's house at just after ten o'clock last night, but she never made it home. Witnesses report seeing the girl walking along Broad Street, only a few blocks from her house, but there the trail ends.

> Sandy is the second child to vanish in the last two days, leading the authorities to fear about the worst.
>
> "My prayer is that both of these young ladies will return home safely," Police Chief Wallace Williams told a staff reporter this morning in a phone conversation. "We have no reason to believe that anything bad has happened to these girls, but you can't just excuse the possibilities."
>
> Miltonboro authorities are asking that anyone with information about the whereabouts of Sandy Moxley or Lacy Bennett contact the police department.

#

The article went on to recount the story of the first disappearance and to describe both girls—there were also school pictures of each girl below the article—but Billy stopped reading. He was determined to have a good day, and as sad as the two disappearances were, he knew nothing about it. All reading further would accomplish was to give him more nightmares.

He paused, trying to remember the dream that had woke him in the early hours of the morning, but the details had fled the way those things have of doing. He was fine with that, because they were just nightmares after all. Dr. Miller would have told him differently, but as far as Billy Jones was concerned, a dream was just a dream and nothing more.

"Breakfast's done, hon," Sarah said, and she headed back to the table with two plates, stacked high with bacon, eggs and hash browns.

"Wow, you sure went all out this morning," Billy said. He was unaccustomed to such a large, home cooked meal. When he was growing up, his foster mother had only cooked them large meals on holidays. But that was the price of growing up in a house that kept between five and twelve foster kids year round. "It looks great."

"I'm just taking care of you," she said as she lay the plate down in front of him. "You had me really worried last night."

"I'm sorry about all that," he told her as he jabbed his fork into a piece of bacon. "I guess I just over reacted a little."

"I want us to go see the cops today too," Sarah told him as she sat down opposite him at their small kitchen table. "Sending that photo is harassment, plan and simple."

"I really don't want to involve the cops," he quickly responded, thinking about his conversation with Dr. Miller. "I don't care that you know who I am, but…but I don't want it to get around. You don't know how cruel people can be about something like that." He finally tasted his bacon and smiled. "That's great."

"Thanks," she said. "But don't change the subject on me that quick. Are you sure it'll be okay just to let it go? What if they turn threatening like they did back in Louisville?"

"If it comes to that we can go to the cops," Billy assured her. "But until then, lets just keep it between us, okay?"

#

Sarah Clark was nervous about everything that was happening, but she was determined not to show it. She had a history of overreacting, and it had cost her multiple relationships through the years. But having the son of a serial killer as her boyfriend was a lot to take in. The Peppermint Man Killings had made national headlines in the early eighties, and many people considered Randolph David Jones to be among the worst of the worst serial killers. His name often came up in lists along with Gacy and Bundy.

But when she looked at Billy, she couldn't see any of that. He was a small, narrow faced young man who barely had enough facial hair to warrant shaving. His arms and legs were about as thick as toothpicks, and his eyes were bright baby blue in color. He was smart, but not very highly educated, and in four months he hadn't raised his voice in anger even once. Billy Jones was hardly the vision of insanity and violence that his father's nickname conjured.

As she washed the breakfast dishes, she casually looked over her shoulder to see him staring at the folded newspaper. His expression seemed blank, but Sarah could sense sadness in the way his eyes were set.

Sarah had lived her entire life in Miltonboro--except for the brief four years she'd spent away at college--but she didn't know either of the missing girls. That didn't make it any less horrible. Pine Grove and some of the other bigger cities in the area were known to have violent crimes, but not her hometown. Miltonboro was a nice, safe place to live. The kind of place where many people still didn't lock their doors before going to bed. Even the city limits sign proclaimed it as "A Peaceful Place".

She looked from Billy to the newspaper he was staring at and shook her head. She knew he had to have made the connection, even if he hadn't voiced it. A mysterious letter came in the mail one day, dredging up his hidden past, and then the disappearances started. In any other town she could have feasibly accepted it as a coincidence, but not in Miltonboro.

"It can't be a coincidence," she said at last, and just the sound of her voice made him jump.

"What's that?" Billy asked after a moment.

"It can't be a coincidence that you got that picture in the mail on the same day that the first girl went missing," Sarah said.

"No," he replied.

#

Billy wouldn't talk about the missing girls, the photograph or his father that day, as much as Sarah tried to bring the subjects up. Every time she did, he just offered another noncommittal answer and started talking about something else. It almost seemed to her that he was doing so without thinking about it, as if some part of his mind was unwilling to venture back into the past. She knew he would open up to her eventually, and was afraid what would happen if she pushed him too far.

After a while, though, she stopped bothering him about it and just enjoyed being together. Normally they both worked long hours, and rarely had the chance to go out and do anything. The majority of their relationship had taken place in their apartment complex. After going out for coffee on the night they'd met, they hadn't been on another official date for almost a month. But they had done their laundry together, and several days a week they'd curl up on the couch to watch one of the new release movies that Billy picked up on his way home from work.

It was far different from any of the other relationships she'd been in. As far back as high school Sarah had dated the popular guys, who always wanted to 'go out' but never liked to stay at home unless they were in bed together. Most of those were the pretty rich boys, who always seemed to have the pretty rich friends, and to them she was little more than another flashy toy to show off.

Billy was different. He didn't have *any* friends that she knew of, but it wasn't because he was a weirdo or anything. He legitimately didn't care what other people thought of him. He was happier to sit at home and flip through the channels than he was to be the life of the party. Mostly she loved the fact that he dated her, and didn't feel the need to show her off as if she were a new car.

But that too had its downsides. Sometimes she just wanted to go out, and he would refuse. Now that she understood his past, she could understand why he was that way, but that wouldn't keep her from wanting to go out on occasion.

They started their 'date' at the Miltonboro City Park, sitting side-by-side on the bank of Raven Creek, holding hands. Soon after they'd set down, a doe and her fawn came running out of the bushes and stopped to drink just a few feet away. It was the most romantic thing she'd seen, outside of the movies.

When they were tired of sitting in one place, they walked along the creek for a while, and finally headed back into town for lunch. After a quick meal at McDonalds, they headed to the movies. The film was something the critics praised, but they didn't care. They weren't planning on paying much attention to what was on the screen anyway.

For dinner they went to O'Doul's, an odd Irish-pub-by-night, Italian restaurant-by-day type of place that can only be found in small towns. It offered both surprisingly good food, and surprisingly good beer. They spent the evening eating and chatting in the dim candle light.

When eight o'clock rolled around and they were still sitting there, Sarah suggested they go into the bar area.

#

As soon as they stepped into the smoke filled bar, he spotted the group from Phil's Auto Mart. James Jenkins, another mechanic, was standing in his chair belting out the chorus of an old country song. Three or four other guys from the garage were laughing and cheering him on. The table was littered with empty beer bottles and smoking cigarettes. Billy paused, wondering if coming to the bar was the right idea. Then he bit his lip, stuck his chest out and walked into the room.

His co-workers welcomed them with open arms and free beer. As expected, however, the conversation eventually turned to the drain plug. Sarah looked at him nervously, probably looking to see if he was going to relapse into the state he'd been in the night before, but Billy tried to shake it off.

"Dude, he was so mad," James Jenkins said. He slapped his knee and started laughing. "I've never seen Phil turn that shade of red."

Oh God, Billy thought. *I'm gonna get fired over this.*

Tim Wilson shook his head as he laughed along with the other man. "Don't worry about it, bubba," he said at last. "Phil gets mad from time to time, but he'll be okay tomorrow.

I think we've all messed up somewhere along the way. Heck, Phil sent a car out of there a few years ago without any break fluid in it." Everyone broke out in laughter again, and Billy nervously laughed along with them. "You should have seen his face after that one."

"I don't want to get fired," he said.

"Really, kid, don't worry about it," one of the other mechanics said.

"He was pretty angry though," Billy said.

"That's his way, Billy," Wilson assured him. "He gets mad easy, and then he forgives easily. You're a great mechanic, kid. Just make sure you don't do it again tomorrow."

"I'm sure he won't be too happy about me yelling at him."

The rest of the group shrugged, and someone ordered another round. Sarah squeezed Billy's hand beneath the table, and he forced a smile. But he didn't feel like smiling. He really could lose this job, and if that happened, he didn't know what he would do. Miltonboro was a small town, and Phil's was the only garage in town, not counting the one or two person shade tree mechanics that continually undercut their prices. The nearest full-sized service station was in Pine Grove at the Chevrolet dealership, more than a half hour away.

He tried not to think about work. Instead he focused his attention on downing one beer after another, and regretting having let Sarah talk him into visiting the bar. Drinking wasn't really his idea of fun, although he and his former roommates had gone on a few benders back in California, and drinking with people he didn't really know just made it worse.

Billy tried not to pay attention to the worried looks his girlfriend kept throwing his way, but it was hard. He wished he could bring himself to get mad at her for not letting him suffer in his own way, but he couldn't. Sarah was just worried about him, and it had been a very long time since he'd had someone worry about him.

Sometime later everything seemed to blur. He was no longer aware of the way Sarah was looking at him, and he'd lost all track of the conversations going on around the table. He even smiled a little, proud that he'd drank himself into oblivion. Billy had spent most of his life on the verge of a panic attack, and having even a moment where nothing bothered him was a blessing. He might suffer from it in the morning, but in the moment it felt wonderful. He felt free.

Then a strong hand gripped him by the shoulder, squeezing until it started to hurt. Billy bolted to his feet and spun drunkenly towards his assailant. Emmitt Dixon grinned at him. Jackson had never thought much of the man before, but in faded blue jeans and a sleeveless t-shirt, he looked surprisingly tough. He also looked more than a little drunk, and ready to fight.

"What's up, Emmitt!" Jenkins yelled from across the table. The man's words word slurred, and when he moved to wave to the new arrival, he only succeeded in sloshing his beer onto the people seated around him, and knocking a salt shaker to the floor. It burst, spilling salt and glass everywhere.

But Dixon's attention never wavered. He leaned threateningly into Billy's face, and once again grabbed the younger man's shoulder. He bared a mouthful of crooked teeth in a predatory grin. Billy Jackson shifted nervously. He had never been a fighter. In fact, he was the boy in middle school who was regularly rewarded with swirllies because he wouldn't fight. After a decade of growing up, he was suddenly turned back into that wimpy little boy, and Emmitt was the school bully.

"What're you doing here?" the man demanded.

"Just…just drinking with the rest of the guys."

"We don't like your kind here," Dixon said.

"Billy, lets just go," Sarah said, gently grabbing at his arm.

Billy shrugged her hand off and smiled, trying to equal the look on the other man's face. "Oh, and what kind is that?" he snapped. He wasn't going to be pushed around by another bully, even if that bully was his supervisor. "If you have something to say to me, then say it."

"Shut up, boy," Emmitt said. He shoved Billy backwards, almost knocking him onto the table. The whole room seemed to go quiet in anticipation of the coming fight. A few of their co-workers voiced half-hearted protests. "I didn't come here to listen to you jabber. I came here to drink and kick some butt."

He drunkenly drew back to swing, and Billy Jackson hit him with a quick jab to the eye. Caught off guard, Dixon stumbled backwards, hit a chair and landed on his backside. He stared drunkenly down at his own feet, and then gawked at the younger man. As he stumbled back to his feet, his face twisted into a hateful glare. Before he had the chance to attack, Billy went after him, landing another punch to the man's stomach. The head mechanic side-stepped a third punch, and brought his fists down on Billy's neck.

Billy's vision flashed white, and he stumbled and fell to is knees. One booted foot kicked him in the face, busting his lip. A second later the foot returned and collided with his ribs, knocking the wind out of him. His left side exploded in pain. He rolled to the side and kicked out blindly. He connected solidly with Emmitt Dixon's left knee, and the man joined him on the floor with a squeal of pain, which was followed by a stream of slurred curses.

"Billy lets go!" Sarah demanded, and although he knew she'd spoken, he didn't really hear her. He was staring at Emmitt, who in his mind suddenly looked like every bully that had ever stole his lunch money or knocked his school books out of his hands.

Billy lunged forward, through the bursting pain in his side, drawing on a pool of anger that he hadn't known he possessed. He came down atop the other man, his hands clawing at Emmitt's throat. His supervisor's eyes went wide, and then he was trying to pull the younger, smaller man's hands away. But Billy wasn't having it. He had twenty-four years of anger and sadness that needed to come out, and it was all coming out through his hands as they choked the life out of his supervisor.

There was a loud commotion from somewhere outside of Billy's line—of—sight, and two very large bouncers appeared. One of them punched Billy hard in the side, and the boy's hands let go of Emmitt. Each one of the bouncers grabbed one of the fighters and dragged him towards an exit.

"Good fight, Ali," Jenkins yelled after them. Billy wasn't quite sure which of them the man was yelling at, but he didn't think it mattered. James Jenkins himself was probably too drunk to know.

A pot bellied man in a t-shirt and leather vest came storming out of the back of the bar, a wooden baseball bat in his hand. He looked at the two fighters, his face twisted into a scowl. He pointed his weapon at the two of them, and seemed to be searching for the right words.

At last he cursed and told them, "I don't need this. I run a respectable business here, and I don't need hoodlums like you messing everything up for me." He turned to the bouncers and threw his arms up in the air. "Get them out of here."

As his bouncer deposited Billy in a puddle outside the front door, the young mechanic smiled. It was the first time he'd ever stood up for himself against a bully. That alone was worth the trip to Murray's. He pressed the back of his hand to his mouth, and it came away bloody. He laughed and struggled to his feet. The bouncer stared wordlessly after him, watching to make sure there were no more problems between the two drunks. There wasn't.

Billy Jackson tried to get to his feet, but only managed to thrash about in the mud puddle, covering his clothes in dark water. Sarah grabbed him by the arm and helped him to his feet. He braced himself between his girlfriend and a parked Ford Escort and stared at his opponent.

Emmitt Dixon stumbled towards his rusty pickup, which was parked crooked across two different parking spaces. He took one last look towards Billy and threw up his middle finger.

"You're a mess, Billy," Sarah said, trying to pull him towards his truck. He shook her arm off, then fell back into a mud puddle.

Chapter Five

The phone woke Billy the next morning. He opened his eyes, expecting to be greeted by a headache, but he was surprised to find that his head felt exceptionally clear. Normally if he drank more than a couple of beers, he was destined to awake with a hangover. This time he wouldn't have even known he'd been drunk, if it wasn't for the morning after taste in his mouth--the foul taste of cigarettes and beer.

Then phone rang again, and he grabbed the handset from his nightstand. "Hello?" he asked.

"Billy, this is Phil," his boss said from the other end. "Can you come in for a few minutes this morning? We have a few things we need to talk about."

"Uh, yes sir," Billy responded. "When do you want to see me?"

"I've got meetings all afternoon, so if you can get here in the next hour, that would be great," Phil Butler told him.

"I'll be there, sir."

After he'd hung up, Billy got out of bed and headed for his closet. He quickly pulled on a clean shirt and a reasonably clean pair of jeans. Then he headed into the kitchen, where Sarah had left a note, weighted down by a bottle of ketchup. It simply said: *We need to talk later.*

Billy stepped outside to dark skies and pounding rain. Occasionally a bolt of lightening or a crackle of thunder would break the monotony of the downpour, but mostly it rained. He returned to the living room closet, where he donned a raincoat and was off to the garage, his near breakdown of the previous day forgotten. Once again he left the radio off, as a precaution. He didn't want to break the mood. Sometimes his mental state was volatile, and he didn't want to send himself off on another trip. His night at the bar with his new friends had left him feeling good, and he wasn't going to let it be spoiled. He even managed a small smile as he looked up at the dark sky.

He was used to arriving at the garage early in the mornings, so when he pulled into the lot near midday, Billy had to make two trips around the lot before he could find a parking spot. He ended up near the very end of the lot and had to walk nearly a hundred yards in the rain, which was beginning to pickup.

James Jenkins, who was smoking a cigarette just inside one of the garage's open bay doors, raised his hand in salute. Billy returned the wave and smiled. The regret he'd felt the night before about joining his coworkers in the bar had faded, and after sleeping it off, he was actually glad he'd spent some time with them. It would be nice to have some friends for a change.

"How you fill this morning, slugger?" the other man asked.

"Surprisingly good," Billy said. He ducked into the garage, out of the rain. "I hope Emmitt feels a lot worse than I do."

"Well, he's been locked up in his office all morning," Jenkins told him. He flicked his Marlboro out into the rain. "But he looked pretty rough when he came in, about an hour late." He smiled and slapped the younger man on the back. "Man, that was the greatest thing I've ever seen. Me and the boys loved it. S'about time somebody put that guy in his place."

Billy nodded in agreement. "I guess I'd better get in to see Phil," he told his new friend. "Keep your fingers crossed."

Billy headed for the boss's office, as James Jenkins started back towards the oil change pit. He suddenly had butterflies in his stomach. This meeting could very well decide his future at the Auto Mart.

Phil Butler looked up when Billy wrapped on the glass door of his office. The man regarded him sourly for a moment, and then waved him in. The boy suddenly felt embarrassed, as he had as a boy when he'd been called to the principal's office. He took a seat opposite his boss, his eyes cast down at the floor.

"Heard you had an interesting night," Phil told him. He pulled a piece of peppermint from his desk drawer, and popped it into his mouth. "You're very lucky I talked Emmitt out of pressing charges."

"He attacked me, sir," the boy said. "I was just defending myself."

Butler shrugged. "Billy, around here it doesn't matter who started it," he said. "Emmitt's brother-in-law is one of the county attorneys. He's got a cousin who works for the police force. He's a Miltonboro boy, born and raised. And as much as I like you, Billy, you're an outsider. Most folks around here would rather hear what he has to say, even if they don't like him."

"I'm sorry, sir."

Phil Butler stared silently at him for a moment, and then leaned back in his big desk chair. He sighed and cross his arms over his chest. Suddenly Billy feared the worst.

"I'll be honest with you," Phil said. "I'm not very happy with you because of that thing yesterday…and now I hear that you've beaten up my shop supervisor. How do you expect me to feel?"

Billy shifted uneasily in his chair.

"I'll tell you how I fell," his boss snapped. He rose from his chair, and leaned forward on the palms of his hands. Billy's heart was pounding in his chest. "I think, Billy, that it's the funniest thing I've ever heard!"

"Sir?"

Phil Butler slapped a hand against his meaty hip, and then glanced towards the door to make sure no one was listening in. "Emmitt Dixon is a good supervisor and a better mechanic," he said. "I've hated him and wanted to fire him since the first day I hired him. But he's too good at what he does. He makes me money."

The boy wasn't sure how to respond. He stared at his boss with his mouth hanging open.

"But what do we do with you?" Phil mused. "You can come back in tomorrow, but you're on probation. I know everyone makes mistakes, but I still have to buy a brand-new engine for that car. I guess I could dock your salary, but you wouldn't make a dime for the next four months. So report in tomorrow as usual, but watch out for Emmitt. He'll be looking for some way to screw you."

#

The rest of Billy Jones' day was a mixture of emotions. He was relieved that he still had a job, but he was worried about what Sarah wanted to talk to him about. The night before was the first time she'd ever seen him drink, and he had succeeded in making a fool out of himself. He'd also shown a vicious flash of violence that even he hadn't known he'd possessed.

He could just imagine her wanting to talk to him about his 'drinking problem'. He'd known friends who'd gotten the same talk from some of their other friends, and in almost every case the 'problem' had been one that only the person who'd complained had perceived. And usually it followed a night in which the drinker in question had put down an unusually large amount.

Billy spent the day as any bored person would. He flipped through the television channels until he came to the conclusion that nothing was on. Then he paged through the pile of magazines that had accumulated on their coffee table. When those were exhausted he tried the television again. Finally he stretched out on the coach, deciding to sleep until Sarah returned home.

And then she was there, shaking him awake. She smiled down at him, and he quickly pulled her down into a kiss.

"How was your day?" he asked groggily once they parted.

"Another day at the hospital," she told him. "You?"

"Better than I expected," he admitted. "Phil's going to let me come back to work."

"Even after the way you acted last night?"

"Hell, he and all the guys thought it was the funniest thing they'd ever heard," Billy told her. He sat up as he rubbed the sleep from his eyes with the back of his hand. "But he did tell me to watch my back."

"Well, I would think that was a good idea after last night," she said. "But I don't think last night was funny in the least. You scared me a little."

"So what was the note about?" he asked, pointing to the piece of paper now sitting atop a month old copy of *Sports Illustrated*.

Sarah looked at the note she'd left him, and her face went blank. He tried to tell what she was thinking, but he'd never been good at reading other people's faces. She picked the note up and looked at it as if she hadn't been the one that wrote it. Then she crushed it in her hand.

"I forgot about that," she said, tossing the paper towards the wastebasket in the corner of the living room. It missed horribly, glanced off the wall and came to rest atop the plastic runner that Sarah had been talking about replacing for over a month. "It seemed like such a good idea this morning."

"What is it? What's wrong?"

She bit her lip and her eyes began to water up. Without even thinking about it, he was up and had his arm around her. Sarah folded into his arms and started crying on his shoulder. He gently patted her on the back of the head.

"Talk to me," Billy told her.

"Billy," she said weakly. "Billy, I'm pregnant."

Billy's head began to swim. Visions of his own father went rushing through his mind. How could he ever bring a child into this world? He came from a line of crazy men, and now he was continuing the tradition by fathering his own addition to that line. He wanted to run. Get away before he could screw that child's life up as his father had his, or how his grandfather had screwed his father's life up.

But he looked town into Sarah's tear filled eyes, and he knew he couldn't. He might not have come from a good genetic line, but his foster parents had taught him how to be responsible. He'd gotten a girl pregnant, now it was his job to take care of the child. As he watched his girlfriend cry, he too started crying.

All the bad little kiddies cry.

"We'll be okay," Billy said. "I promise we will."

Chapter Six

"Rebecca Carol joins Lacy Bennett and Sandy Moxley," the morning news guy on Billy's favorite radio station was saying when he got in the truck the next morning. "Local authorities say they still have no leads, but the Kentucky State Police are joining the search for the missing girls. They also ask that you please obey the 6pm mandatory curfew."

He turned the radio off and pulled out of his parking spot. Billy glanced in the rearview mirror to make another check of how badly he'd faired in his fight with Emmitt Dixon. He had several cuts and scrapes, a busted lip and an eye that was probably going to be black by the end of the week.

He shook his head, wondering what his life had come to. He'd not only been in his first fight ever, but his town was falling down around him.

Miltonboro definitely wasn't the town that he'd moved to, and it was apparent as he slowly made his way to the garage. People were moving slowly and nervously, looking at each vehicle they passed as if it could contain a serial killer. He couldn't blame them, because he found himself doing the same thing. An old white van passed, and he wondered if it contained the next John Wayne Gacy—or the next Peppermint Man.

Parents stood at the school bus stop with their children on that morning, hovering protectively within arms reach. The children seemed scared and confused, as if they knew something was wrong in Miltonboro, but not exactly what. He remembered his stay in the basement of his childhood home, and his heart went out to them. Murder wasn't something that a kid that age was mentally equipped to deal with.

Billy also noticed an unusually high number of city cop, sheriff's department and state police cruisers. And no doubt the national media would begin showing up not long after the first body was found. He feared the national media, because when they showed up, his father's name was going to come up. Every time a predator started killing off children, his father's name came up.

It happened in Louisville.

In 2008, when he'd still lived with Douglass Mills and Otis Norris in Louisville, just after the letters and photographs had started coming in the mail, it had started. Five high school age girls had vanished in one month. When the bodies had shown up, the authorities had tied it together.

CNN was the first of the national news networks to break the story, and within hours they had started comparing the murders to the Peppermint Man killings. That was when the letters had turned threatening.

He'd immediately gone to the police, and they had repaid Billy by immediately making him one of their suspects.

Soon after that his friends had kicked him out. When the police finally pinned the killings on a homeless vagrant and cleared Billy, the boy had skipped town and headed for Miltonboro.

"You little jerk," Emmitt Dixon mumbled when they passed each other in the garage. "One little screw up and you're gone, boy."

Billy averted his eyes and went about his business. He didn't just have himself to worry about now. He had Sarah and his unborn child to worry about. Everything he did for the rest of his life would be to keep them safe and happy. Thinking about it made him light headed. He was going to be a father.

"Don't mind him, Billy," James Jenkins told him at lunch. His new friend had joined him on the tailgate of his truck. "A lot of hot air in that one."

"He's pretty fired up," the younger man said.

"We'll you did lay him out the other night."

Mostly they sat on the truck in silence, eating their respective meals. Billy was dying to tell someone that he was going to be a father, but he wasn't comfortable enough with his coworkers yet. So he stayed silent and worried about getting through the day without pissing anyone off any more than they were already. An hour after lunch, Emmitt appeared from his office with a grin on his face.

"Hey idiot!" he yelled. Billy tried to ignore the man, but suddenly Dixon was standing at his shoulder. "Hey, I'm talking to you, boy."

"Can I help you?" Billy replied nervously.

"You need to come with me."

Billy followed him without a word. His supervisor led him across the garage, towards Phil Butler's office. Several of the other mechanics watched them silently, wondering what Emmitt had up his sleeve. Phil met them at the door, and annoyed look on his face.

"This better be good, Emmitt."

"Oh it, its too good," Dixon said. "You two come with me and we can get this taken care of right here and now."

Phil Butler and Billy followed the other man back across the garage towards the break room. Billy wasn't sure, but he thought Emmitt Dixon had started whistling a song. The boy clinched his fists at his side, and felt the anger that had over taken him at O'Doul's come flooding back. He also felt the pain in his temple start to flare up again.

They entered the locker room and went straight to Billy's locker. Dixon turned and looked from Billy to their boss, looking as if he were about to start laughing.

"Open it up, son," Dixon said.

"Do what he says," Phil told him.

Billy shook his head and undid the Master Lock that held his locker closed. He instantly saw what was going on.

A large plastic bag that he had never seen before was stuffed into his locker, and it was that that his supervisor pointed at.

"I've heard some talk around the garage, Phil," Emmitt said innocently. "Some of the guys told me that Billy here had a drug problem, but I wouldn't believe it. I bet he's got drugs in that bag there."

"I don't do drugs," Billy protested. "And I've never seen that bag before!" He turned to Phil. "He's trying to set me up, sir."

Phil Butler pushed the corner of the bag open and sighed. Billy could easily see what looked like a wide assortment of pills crammed inside. He also thought he saw a pipe of some sort.

"I can't believe it!" Billy screamed. "Its ridiculous! He was so setting me up and Phil just accepted every word he said."

"Billy, calm down," Sarah demanded.

"I don't want to calm down," the boy yelled. He felt bad for yelling at her, but the pounding pain in his head was making him lose control. "I want to drive down to that garage and hit Emmitt over the head with a freakin' tire iron."

"Billy, calm down."

"I go down there every day and work my butt off, and this is how he repays me!"

"You can find another job--"

"I don't want to calm down and I do not want to find another job. I've gotta do something about this. Maybe I can find a lawyer. I can sue them."

Sarah grabbed him by the arm, trying to make him calm down. Without thinking, he drew back and slapped her hard across the face. She stumbled backwards, a look of absolute horror on her face. Billy stared at his own hand, trying to digest what he'd just done.

"You bastard," Sarah hissed.

"Sarah, I'm sorry," he said, trying to run to her side. But she dodged away, her hands raised to defend herself.

"You're just like all the rest," she snapped at him, and then walked backwards towards the front door. "Every guy I've ever dated has smacked me around." Sarah paused, one of her hands searching blindly for the doorknob. "I thought you we different. I thought you really loved me."

"I do love you," he cried. "I...I don't know what happened, but I'd never hit you on purpose."

"I'm leaving Billy," Sarah said, and he saw that her eyes were beginning to fill with tears again.

He chased her out the door, but she was already getting into her car. Billy screamed her name, but she drove away. He stood in the rain, unable to tell the rain that pounded down on him from his own tears.

Chapter Seven

Billy awoke the next morning to a bed that seemed larger and colder than he'd ever noticed. A dull pain behind his eyes, and his body felt as if he'd spent the night running a marathon. His muscled ached and his joints throbbed. He felt like spending the day in bed crying, but he knew he couldn't. There was too much that he needed to do. His anger at Phil Butler was gone, and he thought he might be able to talk to the man. He also had to find Sarah and get her to come home. He was lost without her.

He wanted to find Sarah, but he knew his job was more important at the moment. Sarah would forgive him, he was sure, but if he didn't save his job before they brought in a replacement, there would be no chance of getting back to work.

Billy willed himself out of bed and then stopped, staring at the closet. He could see Sarah's clothes still hanging there, next to his own. He decided he couldn't go in the closet to find clean clothes, so he headed for the laundry room. After putting on the first thing he found, he headed back to the work again.

But he didn't quite make it.

Police and ambulance lights flashed from behind a barrier of yellow police tape. The ambulance crew stood around in a circle below an awning, smoking cigarettes. The police officers he could see didn't seem to be any busier.

Billy parked his truck across the street, and stepped out into the rain. A group of people stood on the outside of the police tape, and he thought he recognized a few people from work.

"What's going on?" he asked as he approached the group.

Tim turned to Billy and shook his head. "I don't know," he said. "They won't let anyone inside, and they aren't saying what happened." He motioned towards a car parked in the corner of the lot, between two State Police cruisers. "But that's Phil's car over there, and he ain't been out to talk to us yet."

"What's going on with this town?" Billy said as he settled next to the group.

Finally a big State Policeman came strutting out of the garage. He adjusted his hat and sunglasses-which he wore despite the pouring rain-and stared right at the gawking group of people across the street. He said something to a local police officer that stood nearby, and together the men started across the lot towards them. Their grey uniforms seemed to blend in with the wet asphalt and the dark clouds, making them almost hard to look at. Billy shivered as a ghost of his mood from the previous day passed through his mind, but he bit his lip and struggled to hold it together.

"Officer Tiny Tad Tuttle!" James Jenkins whooped.

The local policeman shifted uneasily and glanced over at the big State Trooper. He looked a little relieved that the other lawman didn't respond. He straightened his hat and tried to look as tough as possible-which wasn't very tough. While the State Trooper could have been the twin brother of the bouncer who'd carried him out of the bar the night before, Officer Tuttle was little. He was barely more than five foot tall, and couldn't have weighed more than one-thirty. Next to the other man his little arms were no more than sickly twigs.

"You folks work here?" the State Trooper boomed. His nametag identified him as Officer Wyatt.

"Yes sir," Jenkins replied.

"What's going on?" Tim asked.

Wyatt straightened his already straight hat, and looked them over. His shaded eyes came to rest on Billy's busted up face, and he arched an eyebrow. He glanced over at his smaller sidekick, who only nodded. The State Trooper pulled a small note pad from the pocket of his utility belt.

"Look like you've been a fight, son," Wyatt said.

"Yes sir, just a bit off a misunderstanding at the bar the other night," Billy replied quickly. He remembered his conversation with Doc Miller, and shivered. "Wasn't anything major, just a couple of guys who'd had too much to drink."

"Uh huh," the big man said as he jotted something down. "Where were you at about midnight last night?"

"I guess I was at home in bed."

"Anybody there with you?" the state trooper asked.

"Not that late," Billy said. "I kind of had a fight with my girlfriend and she took off."

"That's too bad," Wyatt said.

"Any of you have any problems with Phil Butler or Emmitt Dixon?" This time every eye turned towards Billy, a fact that the two officers didn't miss. Wyatt slipped the notebook back into his Batman belt and crossed his arms thoughtfully. At last he said, "Phil Butler and Emmitt Dixon were murdered last night. Any of you know anything 'bout that?"

This time all of Billy Jackson's co-workers drew slightly away from him. Wyatt noted that with a blank expression. Billy saw the look on the cop's face and felt like running. It was happening again. Somehow they had found him and were making him look guilty, just like they had in Louisville.

"I think maybe we need to have a little chat with you, sir," Wyatt said. He pulled the police tape up so Billy could come across. "What's your name?"

"Billy Jones," he said softly. He felt his headache coming back. Wyatt and Tiny Tuttle exchanged another glance, and the local officers eyes widened. "I really don't know anything about this."

"We'll see," the State Trooper said as he spun and led them towards the garage.

Billy's mind was racing as he followed the two lawmen towards the garage. Someone had killed Phil and Emmitt? Pain was creeping back into his temples, and heading quickly towards his eyes. He pressed a hand absently to his head. The previous day's paranoia was threatening to force its way back, but he focused his mind on the events at hand. He had to keep his head clear or they really would think he was a murderer. He had…to focus.

They walked passed Phil's car and into the open bay doors of the garage. The inside of the shop looked just as it always had, except for a half-dozen men in uniforms that were slowly sorting through everything from tools to dirty shop towels. They all stopped what they were doing to watch the three of them as they headed into his boss's office.

As soon as they stepped into the office, Billy's breath caught in his throat.

The place was beginning to smell very bad, but Billy didn't want to say anything. He didn't want to get in trouble. As he sat motionlessly on his stool, he willed himself to breath through his mouth instead of his nose. He stared at his mother, who still lay in the corner of the room. She looked old now. Her face long since vanished, leaving behind a vision that he dreamed about every time he closed his eyes. He didn't think there was a doctor who could make her better. He felt like crying, but he didn't want to make the bear angry.

He glanced at the monster, who was working on something at his workbench. He still wore nothing but a very dirty pair of boxers. His arms and chest were covered with dried blood.

"They're outside," the bear suddenly screamed. He dropped whatever he was working on and started running from window to window. "OH MY GOD they're outside!" He bit his fist and stifled a scream. He turned and stared wide-eyed at the boy. "What are we going to do? THEY"RE HERE!"

Billy heard the crunch of feet on the gravel sidewalk out front. The bear drew back from the window and cursed under his breath. Then he fell to the floor and curled up in the fetal position, the hatchet clutched to his chest like a Teddy Bear. He didn't even bother looking for a hiding place. Instead, he started to whimper. Then the doorbell rang. Several seconds later it rang again and again. The bear whimpered louder with each ring.

For days or weeks after he'd made the girl quit crying, Billy could no longer tell one day from the next-things had been as they always had. The bear left, and returned with another friend. She cried and he took her away. Then he came back with another. It seemed to go on forever, until one-night things changed. He came back alone, and he was scared. They'd hidden beneath the workbench all night, every light in the basement turned out. From that point on, they had hidden every time the bear felt scared-which he seemed to do randomly without reason.

And now THEY had come while they were out of hiding. Billy had no idea who "they" were. Anyone who could scare the bear must be very bad, but the boy no longer cared. They would probably hurt them both if they found them. The boy glanced to the bear's hiding place, but didn't move. He knew he should be afraid of whoever was outside, but he wasn't. The only thing he felt as he stared at the bear was revulsion at the idea of being crammed into such a small place with that thing. Maybe he would be better off if they found him and killed him.

  The doorbell rang again.

  "Hello!" a voice yelled. "Billy, are you there? Billy! Hey-"

  "-boy, wake up," Officer Tuttle said. He was crouched over Billy, shaking him by the collars. He was laying on his back, staring up at the garage's ceiling. "Hey, there you are."

  You aren't a bad boy, are you Billy?

  "No," Billy said.

  "No what?" the little man asked.

  An EMT pushed the policeman aside and knelt over Billy.

  "I'd call that a little peculiar," Tuttle said as he went to stand next to Officer Wyatt.

  "Oh, you think so do ya?" the State Trooper asked. He glanced at Tuttle with a look of contempt, then pulled his notepad back out and jotted something down.

  Billy closed his eyes and-

-woke up in a hospital room.

He tried to remember what had happened, but he couldn't. He knew they'd finally come for him. Billy tried to sit up, but his arms were strapped down. He looked down at the straps and frowned. He put all of the strength left in him into pulling on the straps, but they wouldn't give. He couldn't get away. They had him.

His head hurt, but the pain was far away, beyond the wide chasm created by medication. It was far away, but it was there. He wished he could rub his temples, maybe that would make it go further away, or even stop all together. But his hands were strapped down, far from the source of his pain.

Billy lay back and stared at the ceiling. The air conditioner vent hissed, spitting out sanitized air. It was sterile, too sterile. To him hospital air always smelled like rubbing alcohol, no matter what part of the hospital you went to. Sometimes other odors masked it, but the alcohol smell was always there. Even the hospital lobby and the gift shop smelled like rubbing alcohol. In his mind he'd always associated the smell with death, because so many people died in hospitals. He'd almost died in a hospital on a few occasions.

He was strapped down, which meant one of two things. Either he'd become dangerous to himself, or they thought he was dangerous to other people. After the way Tuttle and Wyatt had been treating him at the garage, he thought he knew which one it was. They thought he'd killed

Phil and Emmitt. Emmitt was one man he wouldn't have minded taking a few more punches at, but he'd never wanted to kill the man.

Or had he? Maybe, he thought, there was just a small part of him that would have loved to strangle the life out of Emmitt Dixon. A part of him that would have loved to watch the man's eyes glaze over as he slowly and painfully died. The same hidden part of him that had come out when he'd fought the supervisor at the bar the other night.

No, he didn't kill people.

Not anymore.

"Hello!" Billy screamed. He didn't know what he wanted, except to make his mind stop heading in that direction. "Somebody, please help me!"

The door to his room quickly opened, and a young nurse ran in, looking scared out of her mind. She took one look at Billy and ran back out of the room. That made him scream louder. He didn't want to be left alone. A second later a nervous doctor in a lab coat came in, a clipboard held out in front of him.

"Good afternoon, Mr. Jackson," the man said.

"Where am I?"

"Miltonboro General Medical Center," the doctor told him. He checked the IV hooked to Billy's arm, and then consulted his clipboard. He nodded approvingly. "You had an episode a few days ago."

"A few days ago?" Billy said. "You mean I've been here for days?"

The doctor nodded. "Yeah, you've been here for about two days now," the doctor said. He looked at Billy, doing his best to look concerned. "Doctor Miller's gone to lunch right now, but I'll see if we can get those straps off when he gets back. You had us a little worried for a while, but you seem pretty safe now. You are gonna be a good boy aren't you?"

You aren't a bad boy, are you Billy?

"Yeah, I'll be good," Billy said. "Who called Doctor Miller in?"

"I'm not sure, he just kinda showed up," the doctor said. He grabbed the bedside remote and clicked the television on. A local news crew was interviewing the Sheriff. "Wanna watch a little television?"

"Yeah, leave it there," Billy said. The doctor smiled, promised to return soon, and left him alone with the news.

"-a suspect, but he is not currently in custody," the Sheriff was saying. Someone said something off mic, and the man's face went blank. "We have no proof that these murders are connected to Lacy Bennett Rebecca Carol or Sandy Moxley. I don't care what someone told you, we don't have any proof of that." The screen changed to show taped video from the day he'd collapsed at the garage.

"The authorities have declined to comment on who the suspect is," a voice-over said. "But sources say the suspect might be an employee at Phil's Auto Mart. We will updated you as soon as we learn more."

A reporter came on to talk about a different story, and Billy looked away from the screen. An employee of the Auto Mart could only mean him. They thought he was a killer! He only prayed they didn't find out who he really was. Someone was already pushing the theory that the Dixon-Butler murders were connected with the girl's, if they found out about his past they'd try to pin that on him too.

"What do they have you watching?"

Doctor Van Miller stormed into his room and switched the television off.

Chapter Eight

Billy turned his eyes towards the window. It was mid-afternoon and the sun was beginning to creep into his room, making everything feel brighter. He'd had enough of the sterilized gloom of the hospital, and was ready for some fresh air. Three days had passed since he'd woken up, and very little had happened. Police officers were in and out all the time, trying to act concerned while politely grilling him about the murders at Phil's. Miller was there all the time, talking about everything but the murders. Other than the cops and the medical staff, no one else came to see him. The rough friendships he'd forged with his co-workers at Murray's had been shattered, and his foster family was still back in Louisville.

And Sarah was gone. Nearly a week had passed since the night he slapped her, and she hadn't come to see him. He knew she was close, because she worked at the hospital, but she hadn't come down to check on him once. He'd called her apartment and her cell numerous times, but she'd not answered or returned his calls.

Van Miller was seated in the room's recliner, looking through a stack of faxes from an associate who was seeing his patients while he was out of town. He looked tired and agitated, but mostly he looked like he was ready to get back to Stony Point. He was the type of physiologist who didn't like to leave his patients in the care of others. Adults could usually adjust, but children were different, as Billy knew. He remembered the first few times they'd met. It had been weeks before he was comfortable enough with the older man to even breach the topic of his problems. It had been years before he could fully open up.

"They think I killed Phil and Emmitt," Billy said. Being out of his straps felt unbelievably good, even if he was still in the hospital. His headache had also gone away again. If not for the soreness of his muscles from all the drugs and two days of being bedridden, he would have felt perfect.

Miller nodded. "Yes, they think you killed those men," he admitted.

"Do you?"

Miller regarded Billy quietly for a moment, and then shook his head. "There's no way you killed anyone, son," he said. "I know you better than anyone, and you don't have it in you."

"I've done it before."

"That wasn't you," the man told him. "It doesn't matter that it was your hands, it wasn't you. He was controlling you. He made you kill that girl. But he wasn't here this time. He wasn't here and you didn't kill anyone."

Hearing that from Doc's mouth was a relief. Even if he couldn't trust his own mind-which he couldn't most of the time-he'd always been able to trust Dr. Miller. If he said Billy hadn't killed anyone, then Billy hadn't killed anyone. The younger man breathed a sigh of relief and lay back on his bed. Miller's words were as good as any medicine they could give him, at least when he wasn't on the verge of a breakdown. When that was happening, nothing was any comfort to him.

"What makes me a suspect?"

"I don't know," Miller admitted. "I'm sure your argument with Butler the day before, and your fight with Dixon don't help." He crossed his arms and gave Billy a look of reproach. "An eyewitness said that you tried to kill him at the bar."

Billy shook his head. He'd been controlling his temper well for months, and then he gets mad right before this happens. He couldn't have had worse timing. Then to slap Sarah and have her take off when he needed her the most. If that hadn't happened she would have been there with him. She could have told the police that he was home in bed all night.

"I was drunk, Doc," he said. "I was angry, drunk and worried about that photograph that came in the mail."

"Do you still have that?" Van Miller asked. "We need to show that to the cops. Someone out there has a grudge against you. Maybe they did this."

Billy had feared that something like this would happen the first time around. Sarah had been right. He should have gone to the police when this first started. Maybe they could have caught the person before they'd come after him. Maybe they could have caught the person before the girls started to vanish.

"How bad have I been the last few days?" he asked.

"When I got here you were flailing around like a madman" Van Miller said. "And you were screaming, a lot. Just like you did back when you were a kid. Back when you used to have those dreams. That's why they had you strapped down. You kept pulling your IV out, and you just about knocked that poor nurse down." He looked at thoughtfully at the boy for a moment. "Have you been dreaming again?"

"Yeah," Billy admitted. "Are they going to let me go home?"

"I don't know," Miller said with a shrug. "If they're going to it'll be this afternoon, now that you've come around. Just as long as you're okay with me staying with you. You're mind isn't exactly in the best shape right now. It wouldn't take much to push you over the edge. If that happens you'll be going back with me to Stony Point for quite a while."

"I feel great," Billy told him. "No headaches, no bad dreams."

Doc shrugged again and laid his paperwork aside. He regarded Billy for a moment and then nodded. "Let me get finished with what I'm working on, and then I'll go see what I can do."

A few minutes later Miller left him to find out when they would let Billy leave. The younger man closed his eyes for a nap, and when he opened them again Doc was back with his release papers. He'd also come back with a grim faced Officer Wyatt. The two men regarded each other with disdain, but Miller defiantly held the upper hand. He'd gotten his patient released, against his wishes.

"I just need to advice you, Mr. Jackson, do not leave town without first notifying the authorities," he said.

"I don't think you need to worry about that," Billy told him.

Wyatt stared back at him, his face as blank as ever, but deep in his eyes Billy saw something else. Something dark. Something that scared him. He knew without a doubt that this man wanted to hurt him, very badly. It wasn't his paranoia sticking its head back up, it was instinct. This big state trooper believed he'd killed Butler and Dixon-and probably that little girl as well-and wanted to make him pay for it. One of the man's hands absently touched the end of his nightstick.

"Let's hope not," Officer Wyatt said. Then he turned his gaze to the doctor. "Dr. Miller, I want you to watch after this young man here. We don't want him to have another 'episode' and hurt himself." His words showed concern, but the tone was accusing. He was asking Doc to make sure he didn't kill again. "We'll be stopping by to talk to you, Mr. Jones. And I think we're going to have a lot of stuff to talk about."

The State Trooper turned and headed out of the room, leaving the two men to stare after him. Doctor Miller cursed softly and slammed the door.

"Don't let him bother you," he cautioned. "He's just trying to get to you. Trying to make you have another breakdown, because that makes you look guilty. And *that* makes his job a lot easier."

"Don't worry about it, Doc," Billy said enthusiastically. "I'm great. I'm happy! I get to go home." But he stared at Van Miller. He didn't feel enthusiastic or happy. He felt lost. In a matter of days his entire world had collapsed, and nearly everyone thought he was a madman. "What am I going to do, Doc?"

"You need to get a lawyer," Miller said thoughtfully.

"Wont that make me look guilty?"

"Maybe, maybe not," the other man replied. "But at least you'd have your butt covered. You're gonna need to do that, I think. These hillbillies look like they've got it out for you."

Miller had barely finished speaking when there was a knock at the door. The two men looked at each other, and then the older turned towards the knock.

Clem Moss was a two-bit-hustler, but he was Miltonboro's two-bit-hustler. As he saw it, that made him one of the town's elite citizens. It had at least afforded him a convertible and a nice country home. His law office was crammed into a small trailer in an otherwise empty lot in the middle of town. His law degree was proudly displayed just inside the front door, for all of those who doubted his credentials-which just happened to be half the people in town. A row of antique law books lined the bookshelf behind his desk, and, he thought, added a little more credibility to his practice. A few years earlier he had taken to dressing in cheap, but expensive-looking suits that often showed up at the Goodwill, believing them to make him look more dignified-and thus worthy of your money.

Moss made a living as the only lawyer and only private investigator in Miltonboro. Through the years he'd represented more than his share of shady characters in criminal court, and helped more than a few women get more than their fair share of their husband's belongings. Some of the latter had actually been fun. Once he'd gotten to pin a false cheating charge on one of the city council members.

He'd followed the man around for months, trying to find some dirt. When nothing surfaced, he'd created it. A few hundred dollars to an out of town acutance had created that picture perfect moment, when it looked as if the fine upstanding councilman was cheating on his wife.

The husband's attorney had tried to argue that he did not know the woman, but who would believe that? Would an absolute stranger walk up to a man and embrace him like a lover? They did if you paid them enough money. Anyone would do anything if you gave them enough money, Clem knew, just as he knew what the judges-and the occasional jury-in Miltonboro would think before he laid a case in front of them. Those two small pieces of knowledge were enough to amass him a small fortune.

At first he hadn't thought anything about the murder of Phil Butler. He'd known the man for years, and figured he'd gotten just what he deserved-Phil had been known to conduct a few underhanded deals in his life, including two near drug busts. But he'd chased the police anyway. You never knew when there was a dime to be made, but anything involving the police and ambulances was always a good place to look. The cops' interest in one of the bystanders had caught his attention. When they'd taken the young man into the garage he'd been fine, and then they'd rushed him out in an ambulance. That definitely sounded like a situation with potential.

He arrived at Miltonboro General Medical Center just in time to run into Officer Wyatt of the Kentucky State police. The big officer stopped in the front door, blocking his path. He stared at Clem as he slid his mirrored sunglasses on, and then hooked his thumbs in his belt loops.

"Mr. Moss," he said. "What brings you out? All that rain this week flood the rat's nest out of your basement?"

"No, I just love running into you, Greg," Clem said with a smile. "Just seeing your pretty face has made my whole day."

"So you're thinking about representing that killer, huh?" Wyatt asked. When Clem didn't respond, the State Trooper shook his head. "It figures. You always were a bottom-feeder."

"Just trying to make sure you don't screw *everyone*," Moss said.

Wyatt laughed as he moved out of the way. Clem didn't pay him any attention. He pushed through the door and headed towards the elevator. The State Trooper had been riding his tail for years, thanks to a divorce-gone bad-at least bad for the State Trooper! But Wyatt's case had been pretty open and shut. Proof of his extra-marital affairs hadn't even taken a setup. Everyone in Miltonboro knew that he had been carrying on with the same woman for more than a decade.

Clem had Billy Jones's room number written on the back of his hand, thanks to a connection he had in the hospital's billing department. He took the elevator up to the sixth floor, and then stepped out into a nearly empty corridor. The only other person in site was an elderly lady, who was strapped into her wheelchair. She smiled at Moss as soon as she saw him, and then started yelling as he turned the other way.

"Ronnie, don't you know your own mother?" she yelled.

"Ronnie's dead, mom," a voice said. A middle-aged man stepped out of a room and wheeled her back inside. "He died in '87, when that-" The rest of their conversation was cut off by the door closing.

Clem Moss came to a stop outside of Billy's room. He straightened his jacket and tie, and then knocked. A middle-aged man he'd never seen opened the door, and he instantly recognized the type. This man was either a big city attorney, or a big city doctor, and Clem was hoping for the latter. The stranger peered nervously around the door, not opening it any further than he had to. He eyed Moss up and down.

"My name's Clem Moss," he said, holding out his hand.

"I'm Doctor Miller," the other man said a little uneasily, but he accepted the lawyer's handshake. "Can I help you?"

Clem produced a business card and held it out. The doctor scanned it, and seemed to relax a little. He even let the door drift open a little further. Moss pushed himself forward, trying to make sure the other man couldn't slam the door on him.

"I thought I might talk to Mr. Jackson," Clem said. "I hear a rumor he might be needed a little representation."

"We were just talking about that," the doctor said. He moved aside so Clem could get into the room. The lawyer stifled a grin and stepped into the hotel room, the sound of cash registers ringing in his ears.

Chapter Nine

The story had broken a lot faster than they had expected. The morning after getting out of the hospital, Billy turned on the television and was suddenly staring at something he'd seen a thousand times; ancient video footage taken decades earlier. He only remembered the front of his childhood home because he'd seen it in pictures and on television a thousand times, but there was no doubt about what he was looking at. A sheriff's officer carried a small burden, wrapped in a blanket, towards a waiting ambulance. Inside that blanket was three-year-old Billy Jones, naked, except for a layer of other people's blood.

"Sources close to the Miltonboro Police Department have confirmed that their suspect is this young man, the son of Miltonboro's notorious Peppermint Man, who killed at least thirty young girls between January and May of 1983," Brent Hickman said. "Details about the murders of Phil Butler and Emmitt Dixon are still being withheld by the authorities. They are also declining to comment on whether they believe the murder of Lacy Bennett and possible two other missing young girls is connected to this case, but the similarities between the Peppermint Man Murders and Lacy's murder are striking."

The footage changed to footage of Lacy Bennett's covered body being carried to an ambulance, and then it showed two quick pieces of footage from the days of his dad's killing spree. All three clips looked eerily similar. As he watched the blur of news footage, Billy had trouble convincing himself that he wasn't guilty of a copycat murder.

"During a four month stretch of 1983, Randolph David Jones, also known as the Peppermint Man, lured unsuspecting girls into this Chevy van with the promise of peppermint candy," the reporter went on as the television showed police searching his dad's old, rusty van. "He then took them home, where he rapped and murdered them in front of his three year old son." The screen changed again to show a photograph of the front oh his childhood home.

"After a six-hour standoff with the police, which ended with Jones's death, authorities located and identified clothes and other items belonging to thirty murdered children, although they have speculated that the Peppermint Man's death toll could be as high as one hundred."

Billy turned the television off and sank into his recliner. His past had finally caught up with him, and it brought a horrible headache along with it. He'd been running from this for two decades, and now it had caught him. He pressed a hand to his temple and wanted to scream, but he didn't-mostly because he kept picturing his father's mad screaming during the last few months of the man's life. He also wanted to cry, but crying also brought back memories from that basement. So he closed his eyes, bit his lip, and tried to force the headache away.

He had lived with the headaches for twenty years, but they never got any easier. They didn't always come along with a breakdown, or with other physiological problems, but each time he had such an episode it was always accompanied by a headache. His mind had always associated them with storm clouds. You didn't always get a bad storm along with dark clouds, but you almost always got dark clouds with a bad storm. He prayed that bad cloud cover was all he was experiencing.

Billy picked up the cordless phone and hit redial. Sarah's home phone rang half a dozen times and then the answering machine picked up. "I'm not here at the moment, leave your name at the beep," she said. The answering machine beeped three times and broke the connection. It was full. It was very unlike Sarah to let the mailbox fill up.

Billy shoved a hand into the pocket of his jeans and fingered the pills he'd been collecting. Doc had given him three pills since they'd come home from the hospital, and he'd pretended to take each one of them, while in reality he'd been hiding them under his tongue until he could spit them out. He knew without a doubt that they'd help his headache, but he was afraid to allow them to slow his mind and body. Even if he was mostly in control of his mind again, the idea that he was being messed with was still there.

He tried to focus, hoping to get his head clear by the time his lawyer arrived. He didn't trust Clem Moss, but so far he was the only local on Billy's side. He didn't want to change that in their very first official meeting by acting totally crazy. His newly hired lawyer claimed to be the best of his profession in the whole county, and as far as the boy knew, that could be the truth. But whether it was true or not, he didn't have much choice. Moss had sought him out, which meant he wanted the job. The way things were going, there wasn't going to be any other lawyers around who would represent him.

"Where's the picture, Billy?" Van Miller asked. The doctor walked into the living room, either not noticing or not mentioning the boy's current condition.

"What picture?"

"The one you called me about, before all of this happened," Miller said.

Billy thought for a moment, but he couldn't remember. The last time he'd seen it, it had been on the living room floor, but everything since then had become a blur. It was possible that he'd thrown it out. It was possible that he'd done a lot of things he couldn't remember during the last few days. He shivered, realizing what that could mean. He didn't want to--couldn't--pursue that line of thought any further, so he just shook his head.

"I don't know, Doc," he said. "Been a busy week." The other man looked at him without any sign of humor. "Maybe Sarah moved it."

"Then we need to find her," Van Miller said. "Any idea where she might be?"

"She's still got an apartment around the corner," Billy told him. "But I don't think she's there. She was scared of me, so she probably went somewhere. Been calling her for days, but can't get her. I guess it wouldn't hurt to go knock on the door though."

Miller looked as if he was going to say something else, but he was interrupted by a knock at the door. Clem Moss walked in, looking nervous and exhausted. He just nodded his head when Billy offered him a soda, and then he sank into the sofa. Without asking the lawyer grabbed the television remote and flipped on the local news channel. They were replaying the same news broadcast that Billy had seen earlier.

"Is any of this true?" he asked when Billy returned with his drink.

"Yeah," Billy said very softly. His eyes were glued to the screen, watching as he was once again carried out of his childhood home, wrapped tightly in a blanket. "Everything is true except the part about me killing those folks."

Moss cursed.

"Will...will you still help me?"

"Yeah, I'll still help you," the lawyer said. "But I've got to know, did you kill Phil Butler? Tell me the truth or I walk."

"No, I haven't killed anyone," Billy replied, but in his head he saw the photograph of Rebecca Haynes that had been left on his doorstep. "I fought with Emmitt the night before, but I didn't kill anybody."

The three men sat silently for several minutes, Doc Miller and Billy looking back and forth from each other to Moss, and the lawyer staring at the television. When Clem had drained his soda he crushed it, and then dropped it on the coffee table.

"Ok, I need to know everything," the lawyer said. "What's wrong with you, to start?"

"Well, you know about Billy's dad," Miller said, waving at the television. "He was there for the whole thing. Every time his dad killed one of those poor little girls, Billy had to watch. He even saw is own mother killed." Moss cursed, and Billy closed his eyes, trying to focus away a sharp pain that shot through his head. "As you might expect, that kind of trauma will do something to a person, especially a small child."

"I would say so," Moss muttered.

"I've been treating Billy for Post Traumatic Stress Disorder and a handful of other mental illness ever since he was taken into the system. It hasn't been an easy process and it wasn't very pretty, but we've just about gotten beyond it...or we had before all of this happened. You see, the human brain is a very fragile thing, Mr. Moss. It doesn't take much to make it snap. What Billy lived through is far beyond what it would mess up a lot of people."

Billy closed his eyes and tried to think of something else as Van Miller recounted several years of his life that he had hoped to forget. He really felt like he was passed what had happened in his boyhood basement. It was the years that followed that were the hardest memories for him. Even a decade later, every time he lay down, he remembered those nights that woken from his sleep, screaming and covered in sweat, and was afraid of what would come to him in his sleep. He still kept most people at a distance, afraid they would ridicule him the way the children at his foster home had.

Clem Moss remained silent through the rest of Miller story. Billy was afraid to look at him, fearing what he might see on the other man's face. Even though he was reluctant to get to know people, sometimes they got through to him. His mind had a way of building up a reliance on other people, which was why Doc had always been a crutch for him. Moss was one of those people. In less than twenty-four hours he had come to believe he needed the lawyer, and now he was afraid the man was about to run out on him.

He massaged his temple, and wanted his medication now, more than ever. But he couldn't. He wanted his head clear for whatever was happening to him. If the cops came back, being drugged out of his mind would make him look even guiltier than he already did. Plus, he still wasn't sure what had happened the last time he'd taken the drugs. He didn't believe he'd killed anyone, but the possibility lingered in his mind. As long as he stayed sober, he believed in his ability to make sure he didn't kill anyone.

"At this point I'm not sure what I can do," Moss told Miller, which brought Billy back around. "There have been no formal charges, and there might never be."

"You can at least talk to them, right?" Billy asked.

His lawyer nodded. "I can do that," he said. "I don't know how much they'll tell me, though. They don't really have to tell me anything until they charge you with murder. Once they do that, however, then they have to make all of their evidence available to me."

"But you *will* talk to them?"

"Of course," Moss said. "That's what you're paying me for. Just don't get your hopes up at this point. If they do charge you with murder, it could be this afternoon just as easily as it could be two months down the road. Our local law enforcement isn't exactly the most efficient group of policemen you could ask for."

"I really don't like this guy," Officer Greg Wyatt said. The State Trooper crushed a peanut shell between his thumb and forefinger, and then ate the contents. "There's just something not right about him."

"Something like killing his boss with a wrench?" Tad Tuttle asked.

Wyatt glared at the policeman for a moment and then went back to watching the building across the street. His unwilling partner clinched his fist and held back a loud curse. The two men sat in an unmarked car, across the street from Billy Jackson's apartment complex. Neither man was on the clock. Both were there of their own free will. The Trooper didn't want to let the killer out of their sight, at least not until they had him behind bars.

"Are you sure we've got the right guy?"

"I'm sure," Wyatt said as he crushed another peanut shell. "He had fights with both men the same day they were killed, and the murder weapon was a wrench out of his toolbox. If you need anymore evidence, just stop looking at me and look across the road. He just hired the sleaziest lower in this end of the state. If he wasn't guilty, why would he be hiring a lower? Especially *that* lawyer?"

Tuttle shrugged.

"Do you even care?" the State Trooper asked.

"If I didn't care I wouldn't be here, would I?" Tuttle snapped back.

"I thought maybe you were just in love with me," Wyatt said. "You've been following me around like a puppy for the last week, and have you done anything to help the case? No! Half the time you sound like you want to let the guy go free."

"I do, if he ain't guilty!"

"Ain't guilty?" Wyatt said with a laugh. He looked at the other man as if he'd suddenly grown horns. "How can you tell me this guy isn't guilty? We've done everything but get video footage of the murders, and here you sit talking about him being an innocent man."

"I never said he was innocent," the other man replied. "I just said he might not be guilty. Yeah, we've got evidence, but I haven't seen anything that proves he's guilty."

Wyatt rolled his eyes and tossed his peanut shell out the window. Tuttle turned and stared out the window, forcibly holding his tongue. He was really beginning to hate the arrogant State Trooper he was sharing the car with. He'd been the same way when they'd gone to Miltonboro High School together. Back then he'd thought he was cool because he played football, now he thought he was cool because he was a State Trooper. Greg Wyatt thought working for the state made him better and smarter than the local police, and he wasn't afraid to say it. He'd forced his way into heading up the Butler-Dixon murder, and would have done all the investigating himself, if Miltonboro's police chief had allowed it. But Chief Braden didn't think any more of Officer Wyatt than he did, and the city police ultimately had jurisdiction over the murders.

"He's the guiltiest man I've ever seen," the State Trooper muttered.

"How long do we have to sit here?"

"Until something happens."

Chapter Ten

They finally went away. The bear crawled out from under the workbench and walked cautiously from window to window. After checking each of them, he slumped to the floor and held his head in his hands. He started sobbing again, quietly at first, and then louder and louder. After several minutes his sobs had nearly become screams. He still clutched the hatchet in his hands, but he looked as if he didn't even remember it.

Billy watched this all from his stool, his face entirely blank, and his mind slowly becoming the same. He was beginning to get a headache. It started deep in his head, somewhere behind his eyes and worked its way outward. Sluggishly he raised a hand to his head and rubbed his temple. Normally headaches would make him cry, but he no longer had it in him, and not just because of the bear. He didn't have the emotions to cry. He felt nothing at, except the pain in his head.

Minutes, hours or days later the bear got to his feet. His movements were as slow and deliberate as the boy's. He glanced at Billy, and then started pacing. He picked some up from the top of the workbench, and then slammed it down hard enough that the shelf holding the canned goods collapsed. Ancient Mason jars crashed to the floor, spilling their rotted contents. A horrible smell drifted up from them, but neither the boy nor the bear seemed to notice. The bigger of the two paced through the food and broken glass with his bare feet, not even noticing the sharp shards that sliced into his skin.

"They'll be back," the bear said as he stepped back to the window. He raised the hatchet over his head and smashed the glass in front of him. "They'll be back! They'll be back and they'll get us!"

The bear turned away from the broken window and stared at the boy. Then he looked down at the hatchet in his hand. A crooked grin spread across his blood-smeared face. He raised his face towards the ceiling, and the basement filled with the sound of his mad laughter.

"Are you a bad boy, Billy?" he asked. The boy sat silently, his eyes unfocused. "Have you been bad?"

He jumped across the distance that separated them, and leaned into the boy's face. His breath reeked of rotten meat, but Billy remained unfazed. The bear grabbed him by the shoulders and shook. He looked back at the ceiling and laughed again.

"You told them how to find me, didn't you?" the bear said. He raised the hatchet over his head, and Billy screamed.

#

Billy Jackson sat up in bed. He wasn't the one screaming, but someone was. The maddening face of the bear suddenly appeared out of the darkness, and Billy jumped backwards, striking the headboard with the back of his skull. As his vision flashed white, the other man vanished. But the sound of screaming was still there, somewhere in the apartment. He threw his blanket off and stumbled out of bed. His knee collided with something hard, sending him sprawling. He felt his way through the darkness, until he found the bedroom door. As soon as he had it opened, light flooded the room. Before stepping out into the hallway he had to look around twice to make sure the ghostly figure he'd seen wasn't really lurking nearby, waiting to jump him.

The screaming was coming from down the hall, in the living room. He limped slowly in that direction, a sharp pain starting in his knee. As he stepped into the living room, he came face-to-face with the source of the screaming. Van Miller was curled up in the middle of the living room floor, his back to Billy. The younger man ran across the room, and dropped to a knee in front of him. At once he saw the source of the problem. A butcher knife had been driven into the doctor's stomach. Blood was pouring from the wound, and pooling on the living room floor.

"Oh God, Billy," Miller screamed. "It hurts so bad!"

Billy grabbed the handle of the knife and pulled. It made a sickening wet sound as it freed itself from the man's stomach. Doctor Miller screamed louder, his hands reaching blindly for the wound. He missed, instead dragging a blood hand across the front of the younger man's t-shirt. Then a fist pounded against the front door. The younger man jumped and dropped the knife.

"Police, open the door!" Billy jumped up and threw the front door open. Wyatt and Tuttle forced their way passed him, their guns drawn. They took one look at Van Miller and spun on Billy. Wyatt grinned and said, "Oh, we've got you now!"

Without thinking, Billy grabbed the handled and jerked the door towards him. It struck the big State Trooper in the shoulder, knocking him off balance. He shoved Wyatt backwards, sending him stumbling into Tad Tuttle. Caught off guard, the two lawmen both tumbled to the ground. He turned and ran, leaving the two to yell after him. He glanced at his truck, wishing he'd grabbed his keys, and headed for the corner of the building.

A shot rang out, and a bullet threw up dirt to his left just as Billy rounded the corner. His heart was pounding wildly in his chest, and his mind was racing faster than his legs. His foot hit a tree root, sending him face first into the dirt. The pain in his knee came rushing back, but he didn't have time to think about it. He pushed himself up and looked for somewhere to run. Apartment buildings and houses were spread out as far as he could see in any direction. He could hear the two lawmen yelling behind him, and knew he couldn't wait any longer. He ran.

He didn't have anywhere to go, but he ran anyway. One of the two people he'd ever really trusted was bleeding to death in his living room. The other had vanished, and probably thought he really had killed Phil and Emmitt.

Everyone else in town thought he was a serial killer. Billy wanted badly to curl up somewhere and cry, but his survival instincts were too strong. If they caught him, he was going to prison, and then probably to the electric chair.

He ran blindly through the backyards of houses. Somewhere in the darkness a dog barked at him, and a light flicked on. He pressed on, not paying attention to anything. Someone yelled at him, but he kept going. He ran through bushes, knocking over anything in his way, leaving a path that even a blind man could follow. He came to a fence, which he leapt over without pausing.

When Billy came down, his knee locked, sending him to the ground again. He landed on a ceramic flowerpot, which shattered and sprayed flowers and potting soil in all directions. Without pause he scrambled to his feet and kept running.

#

Clem Moss popped a Rolaids into his mouth as he unlocked the door to his office. The previous night had left him exhausted and sick to his stomach. He was really beginning to reconsider his own decision-making abilities. He couldn't believe he had been dumb enough to volunteer to be that kid's lawyer. The odds of proving Billy Jackson innocent were quickly getting worse. First he was the suspect in two murders--and a third if the police every charged him with Lacy Bennett's death--now he'd fled the scene of an attempted murder and had become a fugitive. He was also soon to be charge with resisting arrest and assaulting a police officer.

The lawyer froze as the office door slammed closed behind him. Billy, who had been sleeping behind his desk, bolted upright, panic on his face. When he saw Moss, he seemed to relax. The young fugitive leaned back in the chair and pressed a hand absently to his temple. Clem, not knowing what else to do, threw his briefcase down on the desk in front of him, and then stood quietly staring expectantly at his client. He'd learned from some of the rather shady clients who'd hired him to always act like he was in control.

"Bad night, huh?" he asked.

"How's Doc?"

"They think he'll be alright, but he lost a lot of blood," Clem replied. "He's unconscious right now, and might be for a while, so he's not offering his side of the story." He took a seat opposite Billy, and felt nervously inside his suit coat for the pistol he always carried. "What happened?"

"I don't know," Billy said, shaking his head. "I woke up and found him lying in the middle of the floor, stabbed and bleeding."

Clem Moss wrapped a hand around the butt of his pistol and relaxed a little. He'd dealt with all kinds of criminals in his days as a lawyer, but he'd never arrived at work to find a man suspected of being a serial killer sitting at his desk. He would probably very justified if he just shot the kid and let the police sort things out later, but he didn't want to. A part of him really wanted to believe the young man was innocent. But if that was true, what did that mean? Were there killers running around the streets of Miltonboro murdering random people? No, he thought, that can't be true. Every bit of evidence pointed at the young mechanic in front of him. It would be too much of a coincidence for a random killer to go after the boy's coworkers and then his own doctor. Whatever was happening here, it was in some way tied to Billy Jackson.

"Why'd you run?"

"What was I supposed to do?" Billy said. "I knew they thought I did it. That State Trooper was drawing his gun on me. If they'd taken me in, I'd be done. They've spent all of their time trying to prove that I did it, not trying to uncover the truth. I had to run, so I could figure out what was happening."

"So what, you think you're Richard Kimball now?" Clem snapped. "This ain't an episode of *The Fugitive*, boy! This is real life. People don't run around trying to find the one-armed-man. If you're innocent you trust the police to prove you innocent." He threw his arms up in the air and sighed loudly.

"Prove?" Billy asked with a laugh. Then he grimaced and started rubbing his temples. "The last I heard you were still innocent until proven guilty, not the other way around. But the police have been trying to pin this on me from the first time they met me. Can I really trust them to do their job?"

He was right, Clem knew, but that just wasn't how you did things. You couldn't run from the police and expect everything to be all right. He was suddenly glad he carried his pistol with him at all times—at least when he wasn't in court. Staring at this pale faced, blood smeared kid, it was hard to imagine that Billy wasn't guilty. But he'd gotten guilty people off before, hadn't he? He was torn, not between right and wrong, but between his ego and his own safety. He'd long thought that any case was provably in Miltonboro, no matter what evidence there was against the defendant. Plus, in one hundred fifty-three years of history, the town had not convicted a single person of murder. Billy's father might have been the one exception, if he'd not died before he could be arrested.

"I don't know, Billy," he said. "I really don't. As I've said, I don't have much respect for local law enforcement, but you can't keep running away from this. The longer you're on the street, the more it looks like you're guilty. And if you seem like a threat, they won't hesitate to shoot you."

"Then what do I do?" the boy asked. He suddenly looked sick and defeated. His shoulders sank and his eyes seemed to glaze over. "You're the only one I know here, Clem, now that Doc's in the hospital and Sarah's left me. And I've only known you for a couple of days. What do I do?"

"You can give yourself up."

"That's not an option," Billy said.

"Then I don't know what else you can do." Clem said. "Maybe I can find Sarah. Do you have any idea where she could be?"

"I don't know," Billy told him.

"Well, I'll do what I can," the lawyer said. "I don't want you to go near her, because if they know about her, they'll be watching for you."

Billy sighed heavily. He stopped rubbing his temple and leaned forward in the chair. He stared at his lawyer with eyes that were suddenly intense. Clem shifted uneasily and tightened the grip on his gun. Then, for several moments, the two men sat there silently, staring uncomfortably into each other's eyes.

"If I turn myself in, they'll convict me."

"If you don't turn yourself in they'll kill you."

Billy blinked, then turned his gaze to the old work carpet beneath their feet. "I would rather be dead, than falsely convicted and locked up on death row," he said. "They'll kill me there too, it'll just take a lot longer. Its best, I think, if they get it over with quickly."

"Don't you go and do nothing stupid," Moss cautioned, all the time aware of the gun's weight in his hand. He needed to pop another Rolaid to fight the acid building up in his stomach, but he was afraid any movement might set the boy off. "We've still got a chance here, if you'll just play it smart."

"Smart," Billy said with a laugh. "I think it's a little too late to be smart. I assaulted a cop last night, and I left a bloody knife at the crime scene with my fingerprints all over it. That was right before I ran away and got shot at. It's a little too late for smart." He continued to stare thoughtfully at the floor for a moment, and then he looked up at the lawyer. "Maybe you can do something for me."

Here it comes, Clem thought. Here was where he was forced to make the choice between breaking the law by aiding a fugitive, or breaking the law by turning his client over to the law. *Or something even worse, if I refuse.*

Then the cash registers in his head started ringing again. This story was going to be worth a fortune, no matter how it turned out. The son of one of America's most infamous serial killers was sitting right here in his office, running from the police. *Son of the Peppermint Man.* He was scripting the book and signing the check even as he leaned forward across the desk. This case had just turned into something even larger than he'd thought it was going to.

"And what's that?"

"Find out who's doing this," Billy said. "Either I've gone totally insane and have been murdering people, or someone is trying to make it look like I'm crazy. If its the former, I'm as good as dead already. If it's the latter, then maybe we can get all of this sorted out."

"Why would someone try to frame you?" he asked. He popped his briefcase open and produced a yellow notepad. "Who would frame you?"

#

Clem Moss didn't believe him, Billy thought for the hundredth time since the man had arrived. He looked nervous, and kept fumbling around in his jacket as if he were armed. It occurred to Billy that he could probably jump the man and find out what he had in his jacket, but he fought off the urge. This was the last man he could trust. He had to keep reminding himself not to ruin that.

You aren't a bad boy, are you Billy?

Billy shook his head, even though he knew the voice was in his mind. It was quickly becoming harder to separate the little quirks in his brain from reality. This was exactly the way it had happened in Louisville. The real world and his dream world had begun to merge into something else, a dark and sinister world that only he could see. In that world the bear—his father, he had to remind himself--was alive and well, and ready to start killing again. Luckily he'd had Van Miller in Louisville, and they'd gotten him medicated and into the hospital before he could lose track of things. But this time Miller wasn't here was he?

Poor Doc was in the hospital, trying to fight his way back from the brink of death, thanks to a knife that now had his fingerprints all over it. Miller had to make it, so he could tell the police what had happened, but somewhere out there was someone who would have other ideas. Whoever had planted that knife in him would want to finish the job, and they'd do it in a way that made Billy look guilty. He had to get to the hospital, so he could protect the doctor.

The pain in Billy's temples suddenly spiked, and shot through his head like a bolt of lightening. He rubbed his temples and tried to focus on what the other man was saying, but he could no longer follow the conversation. Between the new pain in his head, and his mistrust for the lawyer, he couldn't quite take in everything Moss was saying. He could hear the words, but he couldn't understand them. The man might as well be speaking Spanish--a language the boy had never quite grasped. He stared at a worn spot in the carpet, trying to latch onto something solid, something real.

What he latched onto was a sudden, panicked idea that THEY were coming for him. His breath caught in his throat, and he grabbed a hold of the edge of the desk. In his head he thought he could even hear their footsteps outside, just as they'd come to his house.

OH MY GOD they're outside

"I've got to get out of here before THEY come for me," he nearly screamed.

"Its okay Billy, calm down," Moss said, looking up from a notepad he'd been writing on. "We need to talk about this. What-"

"I said I have to get out of here!" the boy yelled. Billy Jackson pushed his chair back from the desk and stood in one swift motion. The rolling chair collided with the lawyer's bookcase, sending several law books crashing to the ground. Clem Moss gawked at him. "Where can I go? Where?"

Billy leaned towards his lawyer, and the other man fumbled nervously with the thing inside his jacket. He still didn't trust Moss, but he knew there was no choice. He was either totally on his own in a town he still didn't know very well, or relaying on a local man who may or may not want to help him.

"If you're going to keep running, at least let me help," Clem said. "Take a change of clothes and some cash."

Chapter Eleven

With new clothes and a twenty-dollar bill, Billy crept out into the daylight. This would be the hardest part of the day. It was nine in the morning, and the sunlight beat down, leaving nowhere for a fugitive like him to hide. He lowered his head and started down the sidewalk, eyes scanning all directions for signs of police. No one in Miltonboro had known him before this happened, but now his face would be plastered all over the news. Every man, woman and child in the county-if not the state-would have seen him by now. Once he had thought that Miltonboro was like Andy Griffith's Mayberry, but now it felt like something out of one of Stephen King's books. Every shadow concealed some unseen threat. Every house seemed to hold someone who was watching him. It seemed as if every dog in town was barking, and his mind screamed that they were barking at him. The dogs knew he was trying to hide, and they were trying to give him away. He moved uneasily, lost in his own paranoia and not knowing whether what he was feeling was real, or if it was part of his horrible mental state.

He had to get somewhere and hide.

He also had to get to the hospital and protect Doctor Miller, but first he had two obstacles to overcome. He couldn't very well waltz into the Miltonboro General Medical Center in the middle of the day. THEY knew Miller was his only hope at proving his innocence, and THEY knew he would have to come to the hospital to see him. He also had to arm himself, because whoever was after him would be prepared. They would be armed and in hiding, with surprise on their side. Billy had never been much of a fighter, but when he finally came face-to-face with them, he was going to be forced to fight. Without some sort of weapon, he could never hope to win. He was skinny and weak. Whoever they were, they would be big and tough.

You aren't a bad boy, are you Billy

"No," Billy muttered to himself. "No, I'm not a bad boy and I'm going to prove it. I'm going to find them and stop them."

With each step he was aware of the fall he'd taken when getting out of bed the night before. His knee was swollen and pounding, and when he walked he had a slight limp. It also crackled rather nastily every time he bent it. But he pushed on, knowing he had no other choice. He could worry about the pain in his knee when he found somewhere safe to hide.

Billy was also dreadfully aware of the dull pain in the back of his eyes. His head had been pounding now for hours, and it showed no signs of letting up. He longed for the days when he could swallow a pill and have the pain go away. As he moved along Main Street, he pressed his hand back to his temple and started rubbing. Things were going to go down hill very quickly, he knew. He'd gone through this before and recognized the feeling. In a matter of days, or even hours, his mind would shut down, leaving him little more than a screaming idiot. He had to act quickly, if he was ever going to save himself.

At the first intersection he came to, Billy turned off of Main Street and headed into a residential area. With the busiest road in town behind him, he felt a little more at ease. Now he had places to hide, if a police car happened to drive passed or if someone happened to recognize him. The next step would be finding a place to stay until nightfall. He wished that he'd taken the time to familiarize himself with Miltonboro, but it was too late for that. He would have to rely on luck delivering him with a hiding place.

Billy walked at what he thought was an unsuspicious pace, his head down and his hands shoved into the pockets of pants that were two sizes to big for him. He had fallen into a kind of trance, not paying attention to anything, but always keeping one eye opened for signs of the police. Mostly he stared at the dusty kicked up by Moss's shoes, which were old, worn out and also two sizes too big for him. The longer he walked, the further his worries seemed to be from him, until at last he could feel his mind going almost totally blank. He crossed at intersections, not really aware of his surroundings, and he turned down side streets at random. He moved as if he knew where he was going, while in fact he didn't.

Billy jumped when a motorcycle roared passed, startling him back to reality with the guttural roar of its Harley

Davidson engine. He watched the bike rumble illegally through a stop sign, and then accelerate loudly down the street. He didn't know where he was. In the months that he'd lived in Miltonboro, his day-to-day life had never brought him this far off the main roads. He paused on the sidewalk and looked up and down the street. The houses around him came in all shapes and colors, but everything about them advertised the working class status of their residents. It seemed that every vehicle in sight was at least twenty years old, and was beginning to show signs of its age. He glanced at the sky and saw that the sun had crept high overhead, near the apex of its daily route. He had been in a trance all right; he had walked far beyond the parts of town he'd known without the slightest sense of passing time.

You've got to find somewhere to go, he thought to himself as he read the street signs, surprised to find himself near the corner of Rose and Combs-two streets he had never heard of. He scanned the street again, and his eyes fell on a small, one story house a block away. A realator's sign stood at the edge of the yard. Dead leaves nearly covered the front lawn, covering clumps of tall brown glass. A stack of rain soaked newspapers rested on the front door step, and sale bills and junk mail had overflowed the mailbox and started falling onto the porch. There was no car-either twenty years old or newer-parked on the street in front of the house, or under its carport, which had begun to lean to one side. He glanced around again to make sure no one was watching, and started down the sidewalk towards the house. When he reached the unkempt yard, he stepped off the sidewalk and crunched a path through the dried leaves all the way to the back of the house. He glanced in through each window he passed, pleased to see rooms that were bare of furniture and belongings.

From the back door, he couldn't be seen from the houses on either side, and a thick outcropping of trees blocked him from the view of the next block. He checked the door, confirming that the previous residents had locked up before moving out. Then he took in a deep breath and drove his shoulder into the wood. With a loud crack the doorframe gave, and he pitched into the house. The odor of mothballs and dust assaulted his nose, making him sneeze. Just in case someone happened passed, he pushed the door to. With the broken frame it didn't latch, but it would at least look like it was closed.

Billy found a spot in the middle of the house where he couldn't see any window. Once there he curled up on the dusty carpet and closed his eyes. He didn't think sleep would come, but almost instantly he fell into a deeply troubled darkness.

If anyone had been close enough they would have heard him say, in a voice that was not his own, "You aren't a bad boy, are you Billy?"

Part Two

"The Bear"

Chapter Twelve

As night settled over Miltonboro, Kentucky, everyone went about their day-to-day activities with a sense of dread. In a small home on Gulf Street, the mother of Lacy Bennett set an extra plate at the kitchen table, and then broke down in tears. Parents in every corner of town herded their children inside without hesitation. Extracurricular activities at Miltonboro High School were canceled, indefinitely. Clerks working the night shift at gas station and convenience stores had their eyes on knives or guns they'd brought to work with them. A half dozen extra patrol cars cruised the streets, the caffeine loaded police officers behind the wheels watching for anything that seemed out of place. Everyone knew they had suddenly found themselves in an all-new world. The safe, happy existence they had once known had been shattered, leaving all of them feeling scared and alone.

Greg Wyatt stood outside the main entrance of the Miltonboro General Medical Center, carefully eyeing everyone who passed. His shoulder still stung from its unexpected collision with Billy Jackson's front door, and the rest of his body didn't feel much better. He was going on the third night since he'd slept, and his system had been overloaded with coffee and caffeine pills. The temperature was quickly dropping, and his hands ached with arthritis. He rubbed his hands together, trying to ease the pain.

"Nothing?" Tad Tuttle asked as he appeared with a Styrofoam cup of coffee. Wyatt accepted the glass with a nod of thanks, and then told the other officer that he hadn't seen anything. Tuttle nodded and leaned against the wall. He hadn't said much since they'd found Billy Jackson's doctor, and then been assaulted during the boy's escape. "I've got to say, I really thought he might be innocent."

"Live and learn, Tuttle," Wyatt said as he choked down the hospital coffee. It was lukewarm, and tasted burnt. "Now we've got to bring him in before the mayor turns the dogs loose."

They were both worried about that. The mayor wanted to call a town meeting and turn the citizen's loose to hunt Billy Jones down. It was idiotic; it was nearly illegal; and worst of all, if they didn't catch the boy soon, it was going to happen. Hundreds of trigger-happy citizens roaming the streets, looking for someone to shoot. Billy wasn't going to be the only one killed if that happened.

A cold wind began to blow, mirroring Wyatt's mood. He looked up at the clear night sky and frowned. It was much too late in the season for snow, but it sure felt right for it. He pulled the collar of his uniform jacket tighter, and wished for somewhere warm to sleep. But he didn't think sleep would come, not until Billy Jackson was either locked up, or buried.

"You really think he'll come here?"

"Yeah," Wyatt said with a nod. "I'd be willing to bet on it. I just wish his girl friend would show up. I'm starting to worry that he might have done something to her."

"So am I," Tuttle said. "And I know her. She went to high school with my little brother."

Wyatt drained the last of his burnt coffee and tossed the cup into a nearby trashcan. "You watch the door. I'm going to head up stairs and check on the doctor."

The other man nodded, and Wyatt headed back into the hospital. He welcomed the warm blast of air that hit him inside the door, but it did nothing to help his mood. People in the lobby gave him a wide berth-they all knew why he was here. The story of Billy Jackson and his father had broken in Miltonboro that morning, and it was set to break on CNN at any moment. Soon the town would be flooded with reporters from all over the country, and they wouldn't be polite enough to give him his space. The network reporters would follow him everywhere, hounding him for answers. He sighed as the elevator dinged and slid open.

If they didn't have their multiple-murder suspect in custody by the time the national media got here, they would be made out to look like stupid hicks. As the man currently heading the case, that wasn't going to reflect well on him. And neither would the mayor's witch hunt. He'd gone out of his way to wrestle the case away from the local law enforcement, only to suddenly find himself with more than he'd bargained for. The next few days could easily make or break his career, and thus the case was no longer just part of his job. He was beginning to take it very personally. The perfect record he'd struggled to build could suddenly be ruined by some crazy kid, leaving him stuck as a patrol officer forever.

The elevator doors opened on the ICU floor. A tired looking police officer nodded to him as he stepped out into the hallway. Wyatt glanced unapprovingly at the man and the wheelchair he'd acquired to make staking the elevator out easier, but kept his mouth shut.

Van Miller was a very lucky man, even if he was in the hospital suffering from stab wounds and blood loss. If he and Tuttle hadn't arrived when they had, the man might very well have bled to death. Even as things were, he had barely escaped that fate. By the time the paramedics had arrived he had been teetering on the verge of death. Wyatt had tried to chase after the boy that had stabbed him, but he was a lot larger and slower than Jackson.

A doctor coming out of Miller's room almost bumped into him. He managed to sidestep and keep his feet at the last moment. He looked apologetically at the State Trooper, and then glanced solemnly into the room he'd just come out of.

"How's he doing?"

"As well as can be expected," the ICU doctor said. "We're keeping him heavily medicated for now."

"So when can we talk to him?" Wyatt asked.

The doctor shrugged. "Tomorrow maybe," he said. "Maybe the next day. It all depends on how well and how quickly he heals."

"Let's hope he heals pretty quick," the State Trooper said, and the other man agreed, although for different reasons. Wyatt wanted to know all of the details about what had gone on in that apartment building, and Miller was the only one who could tell him. "Just keep us updated on how he's doing."

#

As Greg Wyatt returned to the front door, he once again ran right into his least favorite person. The man face was pale and sickly looking, and his cheap suit and tie were in disarray. He looked at the big State Trooper and said nothing. At least Greg felt a little relief at the tired look on Clem Moss's face, and the coffee cup he held. The lawyer didn't appear to be in any better shape than he was, and just two days after agreeing to represent the killer, the lawman didn't think he deserved anything better.

"Heard from your client?" Wyatt asked.

"I have," Moss told him. The State Trooper noted that the man never made eye contact. "He...called me this morning from somewhere, insisting that this is all a big misunderstanding. He says he didn't kill anybody."

"That's what I would say too, if I were in his position."

The lawyer shifted nervously, as if he had something else to say, then his shoulders sagged and he leaned back against the wall of the building. As badly as he wanted to catch Billy Jackson, Greg felt a wave of humor rush through him at the other man's discomfort. Moss had taken nearly everything he owned in the divorce, moving him from a nice home in the country club, to a small three-room apartment on the bad side of town. His ex-wife had gotten the house, the car and the cabin at Kentucky Lake. He got the dog, and not much else. As much as he loved the little mutt, it didn't mean as much to him as all of the other things.

"Just in case you're interested, he's been charged with three counts of murder," Wyatt said, holding back a victorious grin. "Personally, I want to charge him with a fourth, but we can't find any evidence. Just keep in mind, if it's out there, we will find it, and we will charge him. And I'm afraid there will be at least two other murders to pin on him." He stared at the lawyer to let what he'd said sink in. "When we catch him, and we will catch him, we're going to send him away for a long time."

Moss shifted uncomfortably, still unable to make eye contact.

"Do you know where he is?"

The lawyer shook his head, but Wyatt thought there was something else behind his eyes. He thought Clem Moss knew a lot more than he was saying, and he decided then and there that he was going to hit the man with as many counts of aiding a fugitive that he could. Mr. Hotshot Lawyer was going to find out how it felt to be Mr. Prison Bitch. At this though Greg did grin.

"Finally found a client who won't let you win his case for him?" Wyatt said, no longer hiding his happiness, and feeling a little uncomfortable because of it. Being happy while two men were dead and another was in the ICU just didn't feel right.

"I'll help you in any way I can," Clem Moss said, sounding completely lost. Then, almost pleadingly he added, "I never thought it would come to this, Greg. I really didn't."

Chapter Thirteen

Billy awoke, and was at once relieved to find that his headache had eased. The second thing he discovered was that he was no longer in his hiding place. He was walking very slowly down the middle of Main Street. Cars roared passed, their horns blaring and their drivers shouting obscenities out the window. He tried to stop, but he couldn't. With all of his strength he willed himself to stop, to no avail. His legs kept pumping, and his feet kept throwing up clouds of dust on the Miltonboro asphalt. Without his consent his feet carried onto the sidewalk, and directly towards a small gas station.

Not being in control of his own body was a weird sensation. It was like riding a raft through raging white water rapids. The current carried where it wanted, and no matter how hard you fought, you were still trapped in its grasp. But this wasn't current carrying him down a river. He didn't believe that for a moment. There was someone or something else in his body, pulling his strings like a puppet master. If he concentrated he could almost feel the other presence, a cold and dark thing that seemed to lurk just beyond his own consciousness.

A buzzer sounded somewhere in the back as the door opened, and a young attendant appeared, his hair messed up and his face flushed. He wore a blue hooded sweatshirt with his name badge pinned on the chest. He took one look at Billy, and that color faded away. His mouth opened as if to speak, but no words came out. Instead, he flailed blindly behind himself until he found the handle of a large butcher knife. He thrust it out in front of him, looking like a priest holding out a cross to fend off vampires. Billy heard himself laugh, a strange distant laugh that had never crossed his lips before.

"Please, don't hurt me, take anything you want!" the attendant screamed.

Billy stopped at the counter and scanned the collection of candies on the rack. At last his arm stretch out of its own accord and snatched a handful of peppermints. He shoved them into the pocket of Clem Moss's jeans, and pulled out his twenty-dollar bill. He moved to lay the cash on the counter, and the boy with the knife swung at him. The blade caught him just above the wrist, leaving a nasty gash. Inside his head he screamed, but in the real world he made no sound at all. His mouth twisted up into a vicious snarl.

In one quick movement he grabbed the attendant's hand and twisted. He felt bones in the boy's wrist snap, and the blade tumbled uselessly to the ground. His screaming grew louder and more pained as Billy pulled him over the counter. He knocked over the candy shelf, and tumbled to the floor. He landed so hard on the floor among the Snickers Bars and M&Ms that he was momentarily bewildered, and that moment of hesitation was his undoing. Once again, without his consent, the mechanic's foot rose from the ground, and crashed down on the boy's throat with a strength that Billy had never felt in his own body. The screaming died a quick death, but the man who had been making it didn't.

For a moment he struggled desperately to fight back, clutching frantically at the leg that stood over him. The bear started whistling the old Eagle's song *Hotel California* as it stared down at the man. Blood vessels in the young man's wide eyes ruptured, turning the whites of his eyes red. His face turned dark red, and then blue as his lungs struggled to find air. Slowly the fighting grew weaker and weaker, and finally it was nothing more than a convulsion. At last the gas station attendant spasmed twice, and expired. Billy Jones raised Moss's shoe from the kid's throat, glanced at it for a moment, and then set it back down on the floor.

Then total revulsion filled him, when he realized that his body had become aroused by the murder. It wasn't a feeling Billy shared, but he hadn't shared the idea of murdering the attendant in the first place. His body was acting on its own.

Help! Billy tried to scream, but only his own laughter came out of his mouth. He knelt down over the dead boy and pulled his hooded sweatshirt off. He regarded it for a moment, and then pulled it on over the shirt that he was wearing. The dead attendant's nametag flapped uselessly on the chest, and he ignored it.

"Oh, you're awake," Billy heard his own voice say, but it wasn't his own voice. It sounded rough and almost forced, like it had sounded when he was recovering from bronchitis. "Don't worry; there is no help for you, boy. You're in this for the long haul."

Who are you? Billy asked.

The other just laughed as he dug through the pockets of his new hooded sweatshirt. He let out a cheer of glee as he found a keychain that held a jumble of keys. He raised those keys to Billy's eyes, carefully looking them over. Finally he selected a beat-up old GM ignition key. He started whistling a tune as he turned and headed for the front door, but halfway across the store he fell silent and stop in his tracks. Billy felt his head whip around with a ferocity that made his neck sting. His eyes locked on the butcher knife that was still resting on the floor next to its owner's body. The whistling started again as he bent down to pick the knife up. He then shoved his new weapon carelessly into the sweatshirt's pocket.

Then his hands unwrapped one of the peppermints he'd taken from the candy rack. Billy felt the urge to vomit as the powerful flavor filled his mouth, but his body sighed in pleasure.

Having suddenly found himself a passenger in his own body, Billy didn't know what to do. He struggled desperately to take control of his own limbs, but they continued to do the other's bidding. They carried him out into the gas station's parking lot, and then towards a rusty blue van parked at the corner of the building. He felt his lips spread into a broad smile at the same moment he recognized the vehicle. It was a few years newer, but other than that it was identical to the one his father had owned, right down to the little green air freshener that dangled from the rearview mirror. His hand tried to open the door, but it was locked. Instead of finding the door key, his arm drew back and smashed the driver's window out. Glass cut the knuckles of that hand, causing the other to wince in pain.

And then, for one quick second, Billy was in control again. He dropped the van keys and stumbled backwards. His foot hit something, sending him sprawling on his back. His head came down hard on the asphalt, and his vision flashed white. The pain in his head shot back, so bad now that it felt as if his eyes were going to explode. He clutched wildly at his face, as if he could make the pain go away. He remembered the way the blood vessels in the attendant's eyes had ruptured, and he absently wondered if the same thing was happening to him. He could hear a distant buzzing sound but it seemed to be coming from inside his own head. Then, after one final burst, the pain faded a little, becoming the distant pain he'd felt when he'd awaken in the middle of Main Street.

"Stop it," his voice said, but it hadn't been Billy who'd spoken. He tried to stand, but once again found himself unable to control his own body. "If we're going to have a constructive working relationship, Billy, you're going to have to work with me. There's no time for this foolishness. Just remember, I can hurt you, and hurt you very badly."

As if to hammer his point home, the other slapped him hard across the face. With some relief Billy noted that the pain his fist brought was nearly as far away as the pain in his head. It was a small victory to him, one that he wasn't going to let the thing control his body know. He might hold the upper hand, but apparently he didn't know everything.

Who or what are you?

"Billy, Billy, Billy," it said, and then started laughing. Their body rose and reached through the shattered window to unlock the door. Pain shot through Billy's injured knee as they climbed into the vehicle, but that was as distant as all the other pain. The one controlling him, however, grimaced. "I'm doing all of this for you, and you have the nerve to question me? Surely you were raised better than that. You should be happy that I came and rescued you. So be a good little boy and shut up."

What do you want?

"I just want to take care of business," the thing told him. "First of all we have to take care of that doctor friend of yours. He's dangerous. We don't want his kind pocking around, might cause us some trouble."

You leave him alone!

The thing controlling him laughed, the said, "If you want me to leave him alone, then why don't you make me, Billy-boy? You've never been very good at that before, have you?"

What are you talking about?

"Oh, we've been friends a long time," it said. "If you think hard enough you might even remember some of the fun we've had together."

I don't know you, Billy demanded, but he had a strange feeling that he did. Somewhere in the back of his mind he thought there was a memory or two that could explain all of this.

The other readjusted the rearview mirror, and for a second Billy glimpsed his own face. His eyes seemed to be sunken deeply into his head, and they were a little bloodshot. So much sweat was beaded on his forehead that it had begun to stream down his face onto the sweatshirt he was wearing. Above his left temple was a horrible looking purple bruise, although he couldn't remember having hit the side of his head on anything. Then the mirror was moved, and he was staring at a reflection of the gas station's front door. As the thing controlling his body started the van, he began to whistle again. The tune, although recognizable, somehow didn't sound quite like he remembered it. *Hotel California* sounded rather dull and monotone coming out of his lips. But the other seemed to be enjoying himself, which Billy was obliged to let him do. As long as it was happy, it wasn't paying much attention to him, giving him time to figure out what was going on. At least it would give him time to try.

As the van pulled out onto Main Street, Billy's hand dug in his hip pocket and produced a piece of peppermint candy. The other unwrapped the candy with one hand, and popped it into their mouth. Instantly the strong odor of peppermint flooded Billy's head, having nearly the same effect as drugs. He was suddenly light headed. He felt as if he were trapped in a small room that was having peppermint air freshener pumped into it. It was all around him, blocking or disrupting all of his senses. He had to struggle not to get lost in it.

"I love peppermint, don't you Billy?" his own voice boomed from far away.

What did you do to me?

The other giggled a high-pitched girly laugh.

Tell me, what are you doing?

"We've got work to do, Billy," the other thing said. "And I need to concentrate, so why don't you just relax and let me work, huh? It'll be better for both of us that way." He started to whistle another bar of his song, and then he stopped mid-verse. "You know, you were such a good kid, most of the time. What happened to you? You used to just sit there on your stool, never complaining or anything. Now you're a pain in the butt."

Billy thought he suddenly understood, but it didn't make any sense. Neither did what was happening to him. He let go and let the peppermint carry him away.

The bear paused for just a moment, the hatchet swaying in the air over its head. Billy stared at it, not fully understanding, but knowing that his world had suddenly grown a hundred times worse. He wasn't old enough to understand what death meant, but he knew that he didn't want the hatchet coming down on his skull. Everyone who had met the hatchet had gone away. He didn't want to go away. He just wanted his life to be like it was before the bear came, back when he could still run and play in the backyard, while his mom baked pies in the kitchen and his dad sipped a bear while sitting in the back porch swing. But he didn't think things would ever be like that again. The bear had come and brought an end to all of that.

With his free hand the bear scratched at the bleeding sore on his temple, and this time he winced in pain. For a moment his eyes seemed to unfocus, and the tight muscles in his face relaxed. In that moment Billy thought he recognized his father's face hidden behind the bear's mask. Randy Jones looked sad and alone, and his son's heart went out to him. He wanted to run to the man and throw his arms around him, but he was afraid this was just another of the bear's tricks. Sometimes he did things just to see if he could make the boy cry; it was a kind of test to see if he really was a good boy, or if he was a bad little boy who needed to be taught a lesson. He definitely did not want the bear to teach him a lesson.

Then the hatchet swung down. Billy screamed and threw himself backwards off of the stool, but the blade wasn't intended for him. It struck the bear--his father?--just below the rib cage, sinking deep into the man's stomach. The bear screamed! For the first time the scream wasn't one of madness, it was the scream of a wounded animal. Blood started flowing from the wound, staining the front of the bear's already bloody boxer shorts.

Look at what you did!" the bear screamed, and Billy knew it was the bear.

""I know what I did,""" his father's voice quickly responded. "Now get out of my head before I do it again!"

Billy scrambled away from the bear, but he never took his eyes off what was going on. The creature seemed to be fighting for control of itself. One arm was frantically slapping itself across the face, while the other was grabbing for the handle of the hatchet buried deep in its stomach. It screamed, and the sound seemed to switch between the bear's voice and is father's voice. Billy added his own screams to the sound, not understanding what he was seeing. It was like watching a dog chase its own tail, except this dog was rabid, and intended to kill that tail and everything attached to it, if he ever managed to catch it. Its head snapped robotically around as if looking for some unseen attacker.

Then the second arm found the hatchet and pulled it free, which made the blood flowing from its stomach come even faster. The hatchet swayed momentarily, and it looked as if the hand clutching it was going to let go. Then the weapon swung down and buried itself in the bear's opposite shoulder, the one connected to the arm that was still slapping itself. As soon as the blade found its mark, that arm fell limply to its side. Once again the bear screamed in pain.

Without warning, the fight stopped. The bear looked down at the boy, and then its legs gave. It fell straight down, hitting its head hard enough on the concrete floor to make a wet crackling sound. Its face was turned to face the boy, and as he watched the feature began to change. As the face of his father began to overtake the face of the bear, Billy began to cry. Their eyes locked, and tears began to well up in the father's bloodshot eyes as well.

"Billy," he said softly.

"Daddy!" the boy screamed as he scurried across the room. He fell down next to his father and tried to hug him, which only brought a moan of pain from the older man. "I'm sorry daddy; I didn't mean to hurt you."

"Its okay, Billy," Randy Jones said. "It's okay. Just listen to me for a moment, will you?" The boy nodded. "I've got to go away now. Whatever you hear, whatever they tell you, don't believe it. It wasn't me...it wasn't me. And always remember, I...I...love you."

And then his father's eyes closed.

"Daddy!" Billy screamed. He shook the man by his wounded shoulder, but he did not stir.

Then something happened. It started at the nasty wound on his temple. At first it seemed as if the blood leaking from the sore had turned black, but the liquid began to grow thicker. As the boy watched it formed itself roughly into the shape of a very long, pointing finger, and rose into the air. It drew a circle in the air in front of the boy's face, and Billy watched it, fascinated. Then the finger began to grow, as more and more of the black substance pulled free of the wound. It continued to rise into the air until at last it was as tall as a man. Then, with a wet plop, it pulled free of his father's head.

The thing floated in the air, just in front of the boy, who was too fascinated to do anything but stare. It was still roughly as big around as a man's finger, but now it was over six foot long. The end that had been the last to pull free was split into a dozen tiny tentacles that looked vaguely like the roots of a plant. Each of these seemed to move of its own accord, moving a swaying out in different directions. One suddenly stretched itself out from the rest and touched his father's face. It traced the curve of the man's skull, and then, after a brief pause, returned to its original position. The tentacles drew close together for a moment, and then they all pointed in Billy's direction. One of them--there was no way to tell if it was the same one--stretched out until it collided with the boy's forehead. It gently traced a path across his brow, and then down his cheek bone. When it had completed nearly the same motions it had on his father's face it flew back to its original location. This time the five little fingers began to rub together, wrapping themselves around the one that had just touched his face. When their brief conference was done, the entire six foot long thing launched itself at him.

Billy screamed as the tentacles found his nose and began to crawl in. Then he fainted.

#

Then Billy snapped back to reality. That was the only way he could think of it. It wasn't like waking, when there was a transition stage between sleeping and waking, when your mind had to adjust. This sensation was much different. One minute he was reliving a memory, and in the next he was once again a spectator inside his own body, as fully aware as he had ever been.

The memory of his father's death was one that had remained locked in the back of Billy's mind since the police had come for him. Hypnotism and years of counseling hadn't succeeded in bringing it out of him; it had taken the horror that he was now experiencing to do that. And now that the memory was free, he thought he could comprehend, if not understand, what was happening to him.

He was possessed. Billy could not be sure what had control of him, but he knew it was bad. And he had absolutely no control over what it was going to do.

At that realization, he felt a cold chill that would have made the hairs on the back of his neck stand up, had he still been in control of his body. Everything he'd spent his life believing, everything he'd always been told, was wrong. He's father hadn't been a mad killer, he'd been possessed. Now that possession had moved on to him.

As Billy looked out through his own eyes at the world around him, he saw that they were still in the van they'd stolen from the dead boy. The bear-because that what the thing in his head was-guided the vehicle along the street with one hand, while scanning the sidewalks on both sides of the road. It was still using his lips to whistle that God-forsaken song, while drumming on the dash with their free hand.

What are you?

"Hi there, Billy-boy," the thing in his body said. The bear looked into the rearview mirror and smiled at him. Billy was struck by how rough he'd come to look in just a matter of minutes-or had it been hours? His cheeks were sunken and hollow looking, like those of a man on the verge of starvation, while sweat continued to run down his cheeks in streams. His eyes were like those of a man who'd just finished a week long bender. "Was wondering when you'd check back in. How are things?"

Answer my question!

"Well, I don't think you are in the position to be making demands," the bear told him. Then it started giggling again. "How are things up there anyway? I always found your head to be rather spacious. Not much up there."

Why won't you just answer my question? What could it hurt? You've got control, right? So just tell me what I want to know and I'll leave you alone.

For a long time the bear was silent. Billy took that silence as a good sign. That meant the thing was considering what to do. He wasn't sure that knowing the truth would be of any help to him, but then, at least, he would know what he was dealing with. If he knew what he was dealing with, then maybe he could defeat it and still escape with his life. If not, then maybe he would have the strength to do what his dad had done.

"We are…Legion," it said at last.

What is that supposed to mean?

"It means what it means," the bear said as it turned the van down a different street. "'I am that which always was.' That means that I've always been, Billy-boy. I'm older than time. 'I'm that which always will always be.' That means that I'll always be around."

That still doesn't answer my question.

"It's the best I can do."

What do you want?

"To live," the bear replied, as if Billy should have already known that.

You're a parasite.

"Well that's just rude," the other said, but to Billy it sounded as if the thing was trying to convince itself. "After everything I've done for you, that's how you treat me! Your father would be ashamed to call you his son."

My father tried to kill you.

The bear didn't reply to that for a long time. Then it began to laugh. It was the type of evil laugh that was meant to scare children in old Hollywood movies, but he knew the thing that had control of him—this Legion?—was no Hollywood monster. It was a real, blood thirsty creature and it had total control of his body.

Billy began to hear the buzzing sound in the distance again. He could sense the anger throbbing off of the thing, and if it was close enough for him to sense its emotions, then it was very close to him—close to his conscience. He still wasn't sure how all of this worked, be he wanted to figure it out. If it could seize control of his body, shouldn't he be able to do the same? He let that thought hang in his mind and waited.

Chapter Thirteen

The van rolled to a stop in front of an abandoned building. It had been a warehouse in its better days, but now it was nothing more than a shell of a building. Billy had passed it a hundred times on his way to work, but he'd never really noticed it. It wasn't far from the ice cream shop where that poor girl had last been seen.

What are we doing here?

"Never you mind, Billy-boy," the thing said.

It opened the door and they climbed down from the van. A new looking padlock secured the bay door, and at once it began to enter the lock's combination. When the lock popped open, the bear shoved the door open and returned to the van. It drove inside and then closed the bay door again.

"I found this place a while back," the bear told him. "I noticed it when you were doing all that driving back and forth from that nowhere job of yours. Don't think anyone's been in here for years, not from the way it looked."

You've controlled me before?

"Just been getting things ready!" it told him. "You'd have been in a mess if all of this stuff happened and we didn't have somewhere to go, wouldn't you?"

The bear moved through the darkness with a confidence Billy could never match. Either it had some ability to see in the dark, or it had been here enough times to know the lay out. Neither option seemed very promising. On a dust covered workbench it found a kerosene lantern and a lighter. It whistled while it went about lighting the lantern.

I hate that song.

"Hotel California is a great song, Billy-boy," it said. It lifted the lantern and turned to survey the room. They were in what had once been a delivery bay. The broken and discarded remains of ancient pallets were scattered around the room. In several places the walls had been painted with graffiti, but most of that looked old. "Your stepparents really should have taught you about music. They really had great music back in your father's day."

Don't you talk about my father!

"Billy, don't get so angry, its unbecoming of you," the bear said. They moved towards a door in the back of the bay. "Your father and I were friends. Good friends."

You're a monster! You made him look like a serial killer!

"Oh you have no idea what you're talking about," the thing said as it pushed the door open. A long narrow hallway lay beyond, stretching out into darkness. "You think I made him do all of those things? Ha! That was your old man, Billy-boy. When he stripped those little girls down and slid—"

Shut up!

"Well I thought you wanted to talk. You are the one who brought it up."

Halfway down the hall they came to a door and Billy saw his free hand reach out and push it open. At once he an odor hit him that he had forgotten all about. It was the way the bear had smelt in those days when they were locked in the basement. It was the smell of death and decay.

"Welcome home, Billy-boy," the bear said, holding the lantern up so the light filled the room. The bodies of Rebecca Carol, Lacy Bennett and Sandy Moxley lay discarded in the corner of the room, just as Billy's mother's body had lain all those years ago, and on a work bench in the center of the room was Sarah. Two very frightened eyes turned in Billy's direction and if not for the gag in her mouth, she would have started screaming.

Billy couldn't take it. He started to scream and the world went black.

Chapter Fourteen

The van slowed as they cruised by the hospital's main entrance, and the bear cursed. Wyatt and Tuttle were huddled just outside the doors, carefully watching everyone who passed. Billy heard the distant buzzing sound get louder again as the bear glared at the two lawmen, but this time it seemed a lot louder and closer. He focused, trying to stretch out with his mind and find the thing that had control of him. It was like standing in the middle of a completely dark room and trying to find the source of a noise by searching blindly with your hands. He didn't really have hands any longer—not in the physical sense—but in his mind he was whole. He pictured himself reaching out into the darkness, and just like that, he happened upon the source of the noise. He couldn't see the thing, but after feeling it, he wasn't sure he wanted to.

The thing giving off the buzzing noise was long and slippery, and it pulsed beneath his hands. It was like holding a cold, beating heart. Just touching it filled him with dread, but he knew he had no choice. Billy fought his revulsion and examined the object. It was a lot larger than he remembered it—the size of a baseball bat instead of a finger—but as he ran his hands over the surface, he thought he felt the same shape he'd seen twenty years earlier. He tried to grab it, but either he wasn't capable of grabbing with hands that existed only in his mind, or the thing was too slippery to get a hold of.

"What are you doing!" his own voice hissed from all around him. This was followed by a moan of pain, and the van swerved across the road, almost hitting another car head-on, before coming to rest on the shoulder. "Stop it! Stop it right now!"

The buzzing sound suddenly got so loud that Billy's head hurt—at least the head he imagined himself to have—but he couldn't stop. He'd found the source of his problem, and this might be his only choice to do anything about it. He grabbed the thing again, imagining himself digging into it with his fingernails. This time his grip held. He pulled with all his strength, causing the bear to scream and reach for his temples, but the thing he held didn't budge. He pulled again, bringing even louder screams from the thing controlling his body, and an even stronger explosion of pain in his own consciousness.

"You shouldn't have done tat," the bear demanded. Then there was a sharp flash of pain, and Billy felt himself inside his body once again. The pain in his head was worse than it had ever been, but he was in control again. He threw the door of the van open and stumbled out onto the shoulder of the road. His injured knee screamed in pain, and then gave, sending him rolling down into a ditch. He landed in two foot of freezing cold water, which instantly soaked through his clothes.

Moving was hard, as if he'd forgotten how his own body worked, but Billy managed to regain his footing. He stumbled up from the ditch, and limped towards a clump of woods a hundred yards from the road, across a roadside cornfield. Cars flew passed on the highway, honking their horns at the fool who'd just abandoned his vehicle half in and half out of the road. He didn't know where he was going or what he was going to do; he just needed to move.

You'll pay for this, the bear snapped from inside his head. The voice no longer sounded like his own or his father's. It was what you would expect to hear come from the mouth of Satan, both evil and beautiful. *You can't do this. You can't stop us, no matter what you do!*

As Billy reached the edge of the woods, the already unbearable pain in his head suddenly doubled in intensity. He screamed and clutched wildly at his head, just as he'd watched the bear do moments earlier. Then a tree clipped his shoulder, spinning him sideways. Already off balance from his wounded knee, he went flying into the leaf covered forest floor. His shoulder ached; his knee ached; and his head felt as if it were going to explode. He squirmed in pain, on the verge of fading into unconsciousness. But he didn't want to let go of the hold he had over his body. This might be his only chance to keep control. As soon as he let go, the other would take over.

"What did you do to Sara?"
Wouldn't you like to know, Billy-boy?
"Did...did you kill her?"
She was just gonna get in the way!

"No, please tell me you didn't kill her. Her and the baby..."

Sorry about the kid Billy, but seriously, do you really think you should reproduce? I mean, look at what your father passed on to you!

"Shut up!"

Don't like it, do you? The bear growled. Then it began to laugh. *I can do you as much damage as you can do me, Billy-boy!*

"Get out of my head," Billy screamed into the night.

Come now, that's not what you used to say. You used to like me, Billy.

"I never liked you!"

There was another sharp pain, this time from the back of Billy's head, and his vision began to blur into white nothingness. A heartbeat later the nothingness began to reform itself. In a way it was like watching an artist paint a picture. At first only black lines began to appear in the emptiness, but then those started joining together to make vague outlines. To his right a group of lines came together to form the shape of a one-story ranch style building. To his left a group of lines formed the shape of a large in ground swimming pool. Objects slowly started forming all around him, at first looking like an artist's sketch, and then solidifying into objects that seemed almost real. The first person to appear was a short stick figure, but as it ran towards him, it thickened into the cartoonish shape of a small child. By the time it skidded to a stop next to him, the stick figure was a real little girl, dressed in a pink one-piece bathing suit. She stopped and smiled up at him.

"Hello Susan," he said, instantly recognizing his foster sister, even though he hadn't seen her in years. The last time he'd seen her was... "No, you can't do this! I don't want to see it. Once is enough!"

But you must see it, Billy-boy. You must remember. Remember it all. The bear's laughter echoed inside his head.

"No!" Billy screamed, and tried to clinch his eyes together. But he couldn't. Once again he was nothing but a passenger in his own body. "Oh God, please don't make me watch this."

What's the matter, Billy, afraid of what you'll see? Don't you want to remember?

He remembered the date, although he couldn't remember a lot of details of the say itself. It was June 4th, 2001, and he was eleven. It was the official start of the swimming season, and the official start of the first summer he was allowed to take his oldest foster siblings—Susan Barnes, Wes Clark and Melissa Myers—to the Athenian Swimming Park by himself. For him it was a proud day, the results of months of arguing that he was old enough to be responsible. To the other children it was a day that they could finally run and play with their school friends without worrying about their foster mother watching every move they could make.

"Billy! Billy!" Susan cried. She was jumping up and down and pointing cheerfully towards the other end of the park. "Wes and another boy are fighting over by the volleyball court."

That day Billy remembered having a headache, which the six year old was only making worse with her constant tattling and screaming, but he didn't want to forfeit his first day of near freedom because of a simple headache. The little girl was, like him, the orphan of tragedy, and as such, he felt sorry for her. But a cold, secret part of him loathed her. Nightly she woke everyone in the house with her screams, as her sleeping mind relived her mother's rape and murder. Having been through similar nights himself, Billy understood, but there was a part of him that hated her for it. As a child he hadn't understood, but years later he did. Her screams threatened to awaken memories in him that were far worse than what she'd experienced; memories that he'd been trying for years to hide away forever.

"Shut up," he heard his childhood voice say.

"No, don't make me watch!" adult Billy screamed. "Please, please don't make me watch this again!"

"But Billy, momma told me to tell you if anything bad happened," the girl said, continuing to jump up and down. "Wes is fighting. He's over behind—"

As she turned her head to look towards the distant volleyball court, Billy reached out a hand and shoved her into the deep end of the pool. She was so small that she didn't even make a noticeable splash when she hit the water, and so no one noticed. They locked eyes for an instant just before her head vanished below the water, and he saw that she didn't understand what was happening. She thought it was some kind of joke. But only Billy knew that the joke was on her. He turned his back and walked away, leaving her to sink into the depths of the pool. It would be twenty minutes before anyone noticed the small figure deep below the surface, and by then it would be too late to save her. The lifeguard who was on duty—he was busy flirting with a girl in his high school class—would later be charge with manslaughter, but the judge would let him off with little more than a slap on the wrist because he was still under eighteen. Sick with guilt, that boy would take his own life before the end of the year.

"That's not how it happened," Billy demanded, but he knew better. He suddenly remembered things just as he'd seen them. The memory he'd had over the last fourteen years—the one that said he was in the restroom when it happened—was a lie, one he'd come up with because his conscience couldn't accept what he'd done. "That wasn't me!"

That was both of us Billy, the bear told him. *That was me answering your prayers. The ones that you tried to lock away deep, deep inside. But you as well as I do that killing her is really what you wanted.*

"No, its not," he argued half-heartedly, but Billy knew better.

I think you just like killing girls, it said. And then, even as the memory world around him faded, he wondered what had really become of his girl friend.

#

When the memory faded, Billy was surprised to find himself still in control of his own body. He was sprawled on the forest floor, only feet from the cornfield he'd just ran across. He raised his aching head, and glanced back towards the road. The blue lights atop two police cars flashed, one on either end of the old van. Two patrolmen were walking around the vehicle, carefully examining it.

Thanks for losing our ride, the bear grumbled.

"No problem," Billy mumbled as he struggled to his feet. He kept low, and headed away from the policemen. Until now he hadn't considered what everything that had happened meant for him, but the realization of his situation suddenly hit him. He knew for a fact that the bear killed at least one person while in control of his body, and once they took fingerprints from the van, the police would know it too. He couldn't explain that one away. No one would believe him if he said there was a creature living in his head controlling all of his actions. "I'm in so much hot water."

You can say that again, the bear said, and then it giggled. *You might as well let me take over, Billy-boy. It's the best chance you've got, if you want to survive.*

"You're the whole reason I'm in this mess," Billy growled.

He had to get out of town, he thought as he stumbled through the woods. Every cop in the state would be looking for him soon. But where could he go? Not back to Louisville, they would probably be watching for him there. Besides Miltonboro, Louisville was the only place he knew.

Chapter Fourteen

When you look at the town of Miltonboro on a map, you see an almost perfect square, divided into fourths by Main Street and Kentucky Avenue, which loop around the courthouse at the center. Billy Jackson's house and Phil's Auto Mart are in the North West quarter, while Miltonboro General rests in the southeastern one. Within an hour of locating the van, a combined effort of local police, sheriff's deputies and the Kentucky State Police were gathered in that area, with the help of at least fifty volunteers.

Greg Wyatt crossed his arms and stared as the sheriff gave out orders to the volunteers. The Chief-of-Police, aggravated at his lack of results, had called in the big guns. The case was now out of his hands, leaving him as a lowly subordinate of an untrained, homegrown hillbilly. A report was already on its way to the State Police barracks, ready to be posted in his permanent record. He'd missed his shot, thanks to one little bloodthirsty punk.

Volunteers began heading out, dressed in hunter's orange and carrying a wide variety of firearms. Wyatt watched them with contempt, still not believing that the sheriff was both able and willing to bring in so many civilians to help with their manhunt. It was a great way to get someone hurt, and that person wasn't necessarily the suspect. Having angry people roaming around with permission to carry and use firearms within the city limits was just a bad idea. But that was Miltonboro. The town had an unusual way of doing things.

Most of the civilian volunteers looked as if they were on their way to a pheasant hunt. They laughed and joked with each other as they headed out into the woods. Many of them had been in their vehicles drinking beer before the sheriff had arrived to address them, and were showing the results of the liquor. But the gather lawmen turned a blind eye to the flagrant violation of firearms laws.

Wyatt didn't think their manhunt would turn up anything, except maybe a few injured civilians. He was beginning to believe that Jackson was too good to get caught in their net. He had underestimated the kid back at the hospital. As soon as they learned that Billy Jackson had driven passed the hospital, he decided that he wasn't going to do it again. If the Sheriff was focusing his entire attention on this quarter of town, two-thirds of Miltonboro was almost empty of police. The kid would be out their somewhere, probably getting ready to kill again.

Someone released a pack of bloodhounds, and the dogs raced off into the night.

"Greg, they've found another body," Tad Tuttle said. The police officer marched up to his patrol car, looking as determined as Wyatt had ever seen him. "It was the kid that owned that van over there. He was the night attendant at Jefferson's Service Station. Someone choked him to death."

Greg looked thoughtfully at him for a moment, and then shook his head. "How did we let it go this far?"

Clem Moss was already making his rounds of Miltonboro, his handgun sitting on the seat beside him. The cash register in his head was still jingling, but the sound it made no longer sounded good. It reminded him of how his own greed might have led to the death of at least one person already, and possibly more before the night was over. Of course, he assured himself, once Billy Jackson was capture, he would still sell the book rights.

For him the whole situation seemed strange, as if it was a movie and he'd walked in during the last fifteen minutes, right when the plotline had reached its climax. And somehow he'd suddenly become a member of the movie's cast. He thought he knew most of the back—story, thanks to Dr. Miller and Billy Jackson, but now he had to figure out how much of that back—story was true, and how much of it the boy had made up to make himself sound more believable. And somewhere out there was a killer that he'd not only let go, but had given clothes and money too.

When the cops had found the owner of the van, he'd made up his mind that he had to help catch the boy—or kill him. Before that he'd been dealing with a reasonable level of guilt at having secretly broken the law, but now he had a murder on his hands. Was any amount of money worth killing over? He supposed that once, even as late as the previous afternoon, he would have thought so, but that was before he'd been the one responsible for the murder. He could have stopped it all, if he hadn't been so obsessed with making money.

#

Billy stumbled out of the woods and into the parking lot of a convenience store. Town was oddly deserted, but he figured that was his fault. People tended to not spend much time outside at night when there was a murderer wandering around. His knee was swollen so badly as he cross the parking lot that he could barely get it to work. The crackling sound it made every time he bent it had gotten a lot worse. He had to stop and rest when he reached the building, bracing himself against the wall with one hand.

The bear had been surprisingly quiet for quite a long time, and it was beginning to worry Billy. He didn't know for sure what the thing was, but it was pure evil. And it wouldn't stay quiet forever. It was somewhere in his head, plotting a way to regain control of his body. He was desperately afraid of what would happen if he lost control again. The pain in his head had also dropped to little more than a dull stinging at his temples, but the most important thing was that it was still there. As long as the pain was still there, he couldn't even begin to fantasize that the thing in his head was gone. It remained where it had always been, coiled and ready to spring at the most opportune moment.

"How are things going up there?" he asked, but the bear didn't reply. As much as he feared what it was doing, not having to hear its voice was a relief. For the first time in a long time, he could think clearly. Even the throbbing of his knee was little more than an inconvenience, now that the seemed to have complete control over his body. He didn't care if that control was just an illusion, because as long as he believed it, it gave him a chance to plot his next move.

Billy knew he had to get out of the area fast. City and county lawmen would be on alert, and even the state boys would be looking for him. But just maybe, if he could get south into Tennessee or north into Indiana he had a chance to escape. Both of their existences relied on his getting them out of Miltonboro without getting killed or capture—at least that was how he saw it. Once they were safe, then he could worry about getting rid of the bear. Their strange game of cat and mouse could be played out somewhere that people weren't looking for him with guns.

A police car drifted passed, the roof-mounted spotlights scanning everywhere. Billy jumped back around the corner and pressed against the wall, a second before one of the lights flashed over the spot where he'd been standing. The car slowed, and he silently willed it to keep going. After what felt like the longest minute of his life, the spotlights clicked off, and the patrol car accelerated down the road. He stood where he was, giving the police time to get out of sight. When felt safe, he stepped out from behind the building.

When he was thirteen, Billy had run away from home. He didn't have any real reason to leave his foster home, except maybe the misguided search for adventure, but he packed a bag late one night and left, taking nothing but a sandwich, a change of clothes and a shoebox full of baseball cards. As he walked down the street that ran in front of their house, he was on cloud nine. He was free, and he was on his own. Then, in the early hours of the morning, as he began to grow tired and the desert air turned cold, he wanted to go home. The glee that had filled him after first leaving home turned into loneliness and fear. He'd left his warm bed and loving family, only to find himself cold and alone. It was the same feeling he had as he walked across the parking lot, except this time he hadn't chosen to leave home. At least not in the same way he had the first time.

The convenience store was closed, Billy noted as he limped through the gas pumps clustered in front of the building. During the time he'd lived in Miltonboro the place had never been closed. It boasted 24/7 service, but that apparently did not include nights when the attendants could be murdered. He remembered the young man at the other gas station and shivered. They would have found the body by now, thanks to the abandoned van, adding another count of murder to his list of charges. There would be no way to escape that one. He'd done it—at least his body had—and they had probably caught it on tape.

He froze as his feet came down on the sidewalk. A car was quickly approaching. He turned to watch it, squinting against the glaring headlights. It was an expensive little convertible, and the man behind the wheel was his lawyer.

Chapter Sixteen

Clem Moss recognized Billy Jackson at about the same moment. He locked up the breaks and reached for his gun, but he was too slow. The pistol flew out of the seat, hit the dash and rebounded somewhere in the passenger's side floorboard. He cursed as his car slid to a stop, and he began fumbling blindly for the weapon. He heard footsteps as the boy ran towards the vehicle. In his mind the lawyer saw his client plunging a cartoonishly large knife into the back of his skull. Absurdly, the next thought to enter his mind was that the blood from that kind of wound would never come out of the convertible's cloth seats.

"Clem, thank God!" the boy cried.

He's going to kill me! The lawyer thought as his hand finally found what he was looking for. His heart was pounding as he wrapped his fingers around the cold steel of his nine-millimeter. He brought the gun up and aimed it right at the center of his client's chest, and then thought that he might make it after all.

"What the heck?" Billy said as he skidded to a stop. His knee hit the back bumper, and he collapsed to the sidewalk, out of sight. "What are you doing?"

"I'm taking you in, Billy," Moss said as he tried to unbuckle his seatbelt and keep the gun aimed at the same time. He realized that he sounded oddly like the star of some strange western, where the lawmen drove convertibles instead of riding white horses. *I'm bringing you in, pilgrim.* "For your own good and for that of the people in this town."

"I'm not dangerous, Clem," Billy pleaded, still somewhere out of sight. "I'm in control now! All of that stuff that happened, it wasn't me."

"They've got you on video, Billy," Clem said as his hand finally found the release button. Once he was free he started inching his way towards the side of the car, never taking his eyes from the last spot that he'd seen Billy Jackson. "They've got you on video, and that clerk's girl friend was in the back of the store. She saw everything, and identified you from a photograph. You killed that boy, and it's all my fault."

"No, it's not your fault!"

Clem reached the passenger door, and leapt forward, his gun still aimed in the boy's direction. Billy was no longer there. Where he had fallen was a deserted piece of asphalt. As he stared an empty candy bar drifted passed, carried by the evening wind. *So that's what tumbleweeds look like in this part*, he thought, then shook his head, but he continued to stare after the wrapper as it drifted down the street. Miltonboro did in fact look like a ghost town now that everyone was afraid to go out, although it was in the middle of Kentucky rather than New Mexico.

"Come on Billy, I don't want trouble," Clem said. He heard what sounded like a shoe scrapping the road, and spun towards the other side of the car. "It doesn't have to be like this!"

"I know how it looks, Clem, but I didn't do all of these things," Billy called from somewhere out of sight. "I can explain if you just give me a chance. Please…"

Some part of Clem Moss couldn't help feeling a reluctant sympathy for Billy Jackson, despite the dead bodies he was leaving in his wake. He hadn't experienced anything near what this boy had, but he had lived through plenty of run-in with the Miltonboro Police Department in his younger days, back when he always seemed to be broke but yet had enough money to get drunk six days out of the week. If he'd grown up in the house with a serial killer, there was no telling where he would have ended up. *Probably dead or in jail*, he thought, and then added, *Pilgrim.*

"Billy, I have to take you in," Moss said. "If I let you go the cops are going to kill you."

"I'll run away."

"To where?" Clem asked. He moved carefully across the front seat, watching for when and where the boy would show himself. "There are hundreds of people running all over this town, carrying weapons and looking to get a shot at you. There's no way you're going to escape. Come with me and I'll make sure you survive."

"Survive just so they can kill me?"

Then Jackson sprang at him. Clem spun, trying to get a shot of to protect himself. The boy caught his arm and twisted. Pain shot up the lawyer's arm. For a moment they stood chest to chest, Moss's gun the only thing separating them. The smell drifting off of the boy was a sickening mixture of sweat and blood. His eyes were horribly bloodshot, and there was an infected looking sore seeping blood from his left temple. He struggled, but Billy had twenty-five years or more on him. Helplessly he watched as the barrel of the gun began to drift towards his own head.

He saw something in the boy's eyes that he didn't like. It was the look you saw in a dog's eyes just before it sank its teeth into your calf. There was no way he could be sure what he was seeing was real, but believed it anyway.

Clem pulled the trigger and the muzzle of the pistol exploded. Fire shot from the end of the gun, momentarily blinding him. Billy Jackson's grip on him and the gun loosened, and then vanished all together. Through the spot that was floating in his vision, he saw his client stumbled backwards, clutching at one of his ears. When he pulled his hand away, it was red with blood. His eyes went wide and then very distant. For a moment it seemed that he was staring straight through the other man.

"Jeez, Clem," Billy growled.

#

No! Billy screamed, but his voice was only inside his head. It had the same quality as your voice did when you yelled in an empty room, and for the first time he thought he grasp the size of his condition. He was trapped inside his own brain, which meant he was trapped within the biggest, most powerful "computer" ever made. He was in a world without restrictions, as large and flexible as his imagination would allow.

The bear started to laugh, and then launched his body forward. This time Clem was not ready. Billy watched as his shoulder struck the man hard in the chest, knocking him off balance. Then his hands jerked the gun free. He aimed and fired, hitting his lawyer in the stomach and sending him falling into the backseat of the convertible. He raised the gun and fired another shot blindly into the car.

"I think we took care of that, now didn't we," the bear said. "And we got a new convertible out of the deal too."

You're sick, Billy said.

"No, I'm just doing what you want me to," the thing said. Then it walked around and climbed behind the wheel. "I've already told you that, Billy-boy. Like killing your boss…and that girlfriend of yours."

He could now feel the thing in his head without trying. Its pulsing was like the pounding of a heart, and the angry bees were still buzzing away. Billy was afraid it was getting stronger and beginning to grow. He wondered how long it would be until there wasn't room for the two of them. Then what would happen? It would try to destroy him, that's what it would do. But he didn't think he could defeat it. Whatever it was, it already knew how things worked. If he was going to have any chance at survival, he had to catch up, and fast.

In the emptiness of his own mind, Billy reached out again with hands that weren't there. Once again he found the thing that was the bear, and he'd been right. It had started growing. It had grown to the size of a man's arm. He ran a hand over its cold surface, and felt a cold sinking feeling in the pit of a stomach he no longer had.

He focused, trying to think of anything that would give him a chance. Then he remembered how it had triggered his memory from the day Susan died. If it could do that to him, surely there was a way he could do the same thing. He reached out with his mind, exploring the realm he found himself in. He groped out in every direction, his imagined hands finding nothing but empty space. His mind seemed enormous and filled with nothing but he and the bear.

Billy wondered, not for the first time, what the thing in his head really was. He knew without a doubt that it was a being of pure evil, but that was far from explaining what it was. And he knew if there was one of them, then there were many more, all wondering around the world in the bodies of other people, randomly killing and maiming people. That would, he thought, explain how people like Ted Bundy—and his own father—could do the evil things that they did. Maybe things like this were controlling them all. That didn't make him feel any better though, not while one of them was currently running his own body.

He ran his hands over the bear's cold surface again, and remembered the way it looked twenty years earlier; cold and black with a collection of tentacles at the end.

Chapter Seventeen

They weren't leaving Miltonboro, Billy was pretty sure, at least not until the thing in his head had dealt with Van Miller. The doctor was the only friend the boy had ever had, and the thing wanted him dead. He was not optimistic that he could stop the thing, now that it had regained control of his—*their?*—body. He would try, but he wasn't sure it would work.

Hundreds or thousands of armed men were out there, looking for him. And those men would not hesitate to kill him on sight. But neither would the thing in his head hesitate to kill those men.

Each minute they drove was one less minute he would have to save Van Miller, and maybe himself. Billy would try to stop whatever the thing had in mind, but the longer it had control of his body, the easier it became to imagine the worst. They were cruising through town now, zigzagging their way towards the hospital. If he didn't come up with a plan before then, his old friend was a dead man and he might as well be.

Even if he managed to save the doctor, he didn't see any way out. Too much evidence had already accumulated against him, and even if he had tried to explain it away a judge and jury would just laugh at him. *He wants us to think he's crazy,* they'd say. But he wasn't crazy! At least he didn't think he was crazy.

That was a question Billy had been asking himself since this all started, and he was no closer to an answer than he was before. In fact, the more he thought about it the more he wanted to believe he had gone insane. Insanity could be explained away, but an alien or a demon living inside his head?

The bear had started whistling Hotel California again, and Billy felt like screaming. But he stayed silent, letting the thing get comfortable.

To their right was a cornfield, and when they looked in that direction they could see the gentle bobbing of flashlights. Lots of flashlights. Billy estimated that a hundred or more men were out there, searching for any sign that he'd ran through there. They were headed directly at the road. Those men would all be armed and excited about the prospects of putting a bullet in the head of a man they had never met. His head. Billy felt a cold chill.

Search teams meant either they were getting close to the hospital, or they had had fanned out quickly. The bear switched on the convertible's turning signal and turned onto a single lane road of ancient, cracking asphalt that was little more than an alley. Billy had seen this road before, but he had never really noticed it, the way you rarely notice things you drive passed everyday. He had no idea where it led.

The narrow strip of blacktop passed between two rundown buildings that might have been garages or gas station in a previous life. Overflowing garbage barrels lined the wall of one, and a collection of old junk cars rested along the other side of the road. A man in coveralls stood among the trash barrels, smoking a cigarette, and he regarded the convertible curiously as it passed.

The bear flipped the man off and accelerated. The lightweight car was bounced and jostled as it passed over decades of potholes, and more than once the bottom drug the ground. The line of flashlights were now passing to their right again, except this time they were heading away from the car.

And in the distance Billy caught his first glimpse of the backside of Miltonboro Hospital. He had no clue how the bear had known of this road, but it had taken them exactly where it wanted to go. The closer they got to their destination, the worse the road got, until at last there was more dirt and weeds than their was asphalt.

The hospital loomed before them, from an angle that the boy had never seen. The front of the building had been designed to be aesthetically pleasing to visitors, while the emergency room entrance was fittingly sterile. But the backside of the hospital was as unkempt as the two buildings they had driven between to get here. It also smelled. Before they had even driven into the back parking lot, which seemed to be a loading bay of sorts, he could smell the odor of rotten food that drifted out of the big green dumpster that was parked out back.

Under normal conditions Billy might have questioned the sanitation of a place like this, but he didn't have time. If they made it into the building, all was lost. He reached his hands out into the depts. Of his mind, searching for the throbbing creature attached to his brains. He found it and focused all his strength on getting it loose. His fingers, whether real or imagined, wrapped around the thing's tentacles and pulled.

Get out of my head, he screamed.

The boy felt a quick stab of pain behind his eyes, and then the world seemed to explode.

#

He was suddenly back in his childhood basement, but this time things were different. He was fully-grown, not a small scared child, but all the old emotions came flooding back to him. The bloody man that stood before him was just as frightening as he had been twenty something years earlier, and he had the same snarling look on his face. But it was not his father. Where his father's eyes had been, the thing's black sucking tentacles reached out in the air as if they were looking at him.

"So we come back here?" the bear said, and yes, he realized, it was the voice of the bear and not his father. "You just wont let go will you? Things could be so much simpler for both of us if you would just let me do what I need to do."

"You aren't killing anyone else!"

"You are wrong about that, boy," it told him. "You are deathly wrong about that. As I've said, I've always been and always will be. There is nothing you can do to stop me.

Many have tried to stop me, but they can't. I've been kings, emperors and even second rate serial killers, and in the end their struggles have done nothing but destroy themselves."

As it spoke the face of his father seemed to blend into other faces. Some of them Billy recognized, including on man that had brought one of the greatest horrors the world had ever known. The face wasn't exactly like the pictures he'd seen, but there was no mistaking the small mustache on his upper lip.

With that the world around them began to dissolve, and Billy suddenly realized what he had to do.

Chapter Eighteen

They entered the hospital through a metal door that led to the kitchen. Tomorrow morning someone would probably get in trouble when the police discovered how their fugitive had gained access to the building, but for tonight it served the bear's purposes perfectly.

Billy's body moved undisturbed through the hospital's kitchen, and out through a set of doors into a stairwell.

#

Clem Moss coughed and jerked awake. He felt like death, but he was alive. The bullet is former client had fired into the backseat had hit him in the chest, but apparently it had missed everything important. He pushed himself out of the floorboard, bringing a powerful burst of pain from the wound in his chest. He glanced down at it and his heart sank when he saw how much blood had soaked through the front of his shirt.

He moved to get out of the car and but his body didn't want to work quite the way it was supposed to. Blood loss, shock or both had sapped all of his strength. But he focused and willed himself forward. He stumbled and nearly fell through the open driver's door, catching the headrest at the last second to keep from pitching forward onto the broken asphalt beneath him.

As he moved his chest wound began to bleed again, and he knew it was now more important than ever that he get moving. His head wasn't clear enough for him to realize where he was, but he saw light and knew that meant there could be help nearby.

Clem started sluggishly towards the same door the man who had shot him had used.

#

Greg Wyatt and Tad Tuttle had found themselves back at the hospital again. Miltonboro was a small town, but there were lots of places for a fugitive to hide. So far the hospital and Van Miller were their only leads. It wasn't much of a lead, Wyatt realized, but it was the best they had to go on. If Billy Jackson had any sense he had already stolen a car and left town. In that case there wasn't anything that either of them could do.

The 'volunteers' had swept through most of the area surrounding the hospital and not found anything. Greg was still weary of what those men might do, but the longer Billy was on the loose, the less problem he had with their vigilante justice. A dead murder was a dead murderer, no matter who had put a bullet in him.

They'd taken up their post in front of the building once again, and Tad had sent other local cops to watch the emergency exits. Unless there was a way in or out of the building that they didn't know of, Billy Jackson would not be getting to Van Miller tonight without going through them.

"I'm gonna go grab us some coffee," Greg told the other man.

"I just love vending machine coffee," Tuttle said with a grimace.

Wyatt went in through the automatic front doors and crossed the lobby towards the cafeteria. All of the kitchen staff had gone home for the night, but there was a cluster of vending machines in there, one of which served drinkable coffee.

A pretty young nurse was coming out of the cafeteria as he approached, and he hurried ahead to grab the door for her. She smiled at him as she passed. Greg turned to watch her walk away and ran right into someone.

The man stumbled and collapsed on the floor. When he looked down at the bloody figure on the floor he suddenly thought that he'd hurt the man bad. But a second glance told him truth. He hadn't made the quarter sized hole in the man's chest at first. At the same time he recognized Clem Moss.

#

A uniformed police officer was lurking by the deserted nurse's station on Van Miller's floor. He was turned to face the elevators, which were located on the opposite end of the hall from the stairs. Billy still had no control over his body as he moved out into the hallway and produced Clem Moss's handgun.

Billy had slowly come to believe that everything the bear had told him had been a lie. Despite how it had promised that they'd get away, he thought that this would be the end of their journey. It intended to kill the doctor for its own dark reasons, and then no doubt jump to a new host.

It raised the gun and leveled it off at the back of the police officer's head. The man had no chance. Billy had never fired a gun before, but the thing in his head proved to be more than proficient. From ten foot away it put a bullet right through the middle of the man's skull. His body slumped forward across a computer keyboard, and sent the monitor crashing to the floor.

He heard screams from up and down the hallway, and several people came running out of rooms. They took one look at him standing over the police officer's body in his hooded sweatshirt and disappeared back inside.

"Here we are," the thing said. "It took a lot longer than I would have liked."

They moved slowly forward, slowly scanning the name tags posted outside the doors. Billy knew that when they came to the one that read "Miller, Van R." that they would go in. For whatever reason, the thing wanted his child physiologist dead. It made no sense. Doc was just a shrink, not an exorcist, and he had no idea at all that there was something living in his patient's head. But then again, nothing they had done so fat had made any sense. Killing those little girls was nightmarish, but it had served no other purpose than to give the thing a some enjoyment; an enjoyment which Billy had felt firsthand when they'd killed the gas station attendant.

Unless it got enjoyment out of making him suffer. That realization struck him hard. Whatever this thing was, it killed not just because it enjoyed killing, but because by doing so it was destroying him. First Susan, then Sarah and now Doc! It was killing off everyone he knew, using his own body to do it.

Behind them the elevator rang as a car arrived, and the bear cursed.

#

Mary Sullivan worked third shift, and she hated every moment of it. She spent her nights wiping sick people's asses while most of the world slept. But the hours were more flexible than those of the day shift, and she needed that so she could spend more time with her children. They were, after all, the only reason she worked—that and because her deadbeat husband had run off with some floozy from his office!

Tonight her patient was an elderly woman who'd fallen down the steps of her house and shattered both of her hips. She also suffered from advanced Alzheimer's and tried to hit Mary with a cafeteria tray the whole time she was giving her a sponge bath. But the nurse smiled and kept working anyway; longing for the long imagined day that she could afford medical school.

When he job was done she turned to head into the hallway and found herself staring at a man in a hooded sweatshirt. All she could see in the glare from the hallway light was a shape that looked eerily like the Grim Reaper. She couldn't see the man's face, but she didn't need to. The gun in his hand told her all she needed to know.

She screamed.

#

Greg Wyatt froze when he heard a woman's scream. In the long, empty hallway of the hospital it echoed and he couldn't tell which room it had come from. He dropped to one knee, his service revolver out in front of him. Less than ten seconds after it started, the scream was gone.

Even after all of his training and the years he'd put in on the state police force, he was not prepared for this situation. There was a killer in the building, with at least one hostage. That killer had spent the last week killing people at random. There was absolutely nothing to stop him from killing again except the gun he held in his hand.

Without any training to preparing him for his current situation, he improvised. "Billy Jackson, why don't you come on out?" he called, knowing he was giving his position away. But what else could he do?

#

The thing in his head had begun to buzz again, and Billy took that as a sign of emotion. Anger to be more specific. The sound hadn't exactly started suddenly, because it had always been there, a low rumbling background noise. But when Greg Wyatt yelled out, it had quadrupled in volume.

What's wrong, company would be nice.

"Shut up," the bear growled.

"I didn't say anything," the woman they were holding pleaded. They had one arm wrapped around her throat, and the other pressed the barrel of their gun to her right temple. "Please, just let me go home."

"I'm not talking to you," the bear said, pulling their arm tighter around her throat.

This girl was doomed, Billy knew, unless he could take control. He had done it before, but it was far from a sure thing. They could end up back in his childhood basement again for another chat just as easily as the thing could just pull the trigger and splatter the nurse's brains all over them.

If he fought to save her life and ended up causing her death, would he be responsible? It wasn't a legal question, as much as it was a moral one. No matter what he did he would be found legally responsible for her death, because he had finally accepted that there was no escape. If the State Trooper in the hallway knew he was here, then the building would be crawling with men in a matter of moments. What mattered to him now was how his actions would be viewed in the afterlife. Billy knew it was all over for him, at least he could try to do some good on the way out.

Let her go!

"You know I can't do that."

"I don't know what you're talking about," the woman cried. "You aren't making any—"

This time the bear pulled their arm so tight that the woman couldn't breath. She pulled helplessly at the arm, but it was no use. The thing in his head made Billy's body stronger than it should have been.

Leave her alone!

"I told you to shut up!" the bear screamed.

#

Greg Wyatt heard Billy Jackson screaming at someone, and this time he thought he knew where the sound was coming from. He headed straight at that closed door and threw his shoulder into it. It flew inward, and collided with something soft. He too flew inwards, and collapsed to the floor among a tangle of limbs. Two handguns skidded across the floor.

He could barely recognize Billy Jackson. The boy seemed to half lost twenty pounds in the last two days. His face was pale and seemed much thinner than it was the last time they had been face to face. He was also covered in sweat, as if he just finished some very strenuous exercise. A large, bleeding sore had opened at his temple.

The girl, apparently seeing his State Police uniform as a sign of safety, clung to him. Greg tried to get free so he could go after his gun, but she would let go. Billy, on the other hand, was already moving. He was on his knees and crawling towards the pair of pistols that lay discarded across the room.

Chapter Nineteen

In the darkness of his mind, Billy lunged at the place he knew the creature to be. His fingers found the slippery surface of its tentacles and dug in. He pulled with all of his might, and a sharp burst of pain exploded through his head.

His body collapsed, spilling them to the room of the hospital room. He was aware of the sound of his own screams, but he wasn't sure whether it was coming from inside his head or from the real world. He really didn't care which it was, because it was working. He pulled harder, and the pain intensified.

"STOPITORIWILLKILLYOU!" the bear screamed, and he knew he hadn't retaken control of his body. Then his own fists started pounding on the sides of his head, and the pain got even worse. "I'll kill you! KILL YOU!"

Get out of me!

"I'll never let you go," the thing screamed back. It continued to pound on their head and face. With a sharp crack Billy felt his nose break, and started pouring down his chin. "I'LL KILL YOU, you bad little boy. You're making my head hurt!"

The thing started moving beneath his fingers, as if he held a handful of worms. He continued to pull on the thing, trying to unhook it from his brain. He didn't know if he could ever remove it, but he was going to try.

"I'll kill you like I've killed the Jews," it declared.

The more the thing pounded on their head, the harder it got for Billy to keep going, but he knew he couldn't stop. He would never get another chance. The two of them were heading quickly for the end of their life together, and he didn't plan to go out with a fight. He might lose, but he would fight. Then his head rose into the air, and slammed face first into the hotel room's tile floor.

Billy's vision swam, and the thing slid out of his hands. But he knew he could let go. He flailed blindly and found it again, digging his fingernails into the tentacles. He remembered how it had triggered his memory of killing his little sister, and he focused his mind to do the same thing. He was afraid of what he would find, but it was the only thing he could think of that could stop the thing

#

Flames suddenly replaced the hospital room. He stood in the center of a field of flames that stretched as far as he could see in every direction. All around him he could hear screams of pain, but he couldn't see the people that were screaming.

Then Billy saw them. Dark shapes, withering beneath the lapping flames. Arms clawed out at him, and he kicked them away.

A white light appeared at the horizon, and raced towards him at an unbelievable speed. As it grew closer, Billy found himself forgetting the horrors around him because the light was beautiful. It was like nothing he'd ever seen.

Then the light stop before him, and he realized it was no light at all. It was a beautiful, sexless figure that seemed to glow from within. The form stretched a hand out towards him, and Billy felt as if he was going to swoon.

"GO!" it demanded in a voice that didn't fit with its appearance at all. The voice belonged in the hell that surrounded them. Hell.

The flames vanished, and were replaced by a series of quick visions that moved by so fast that he couldn't keep track of them. He saw gladiators fighting in an arena. Thousands of naked bodies piled atop each other beneath a waving German flag. His old basement. Visions of murder and death far beyond explanation or imagination.

He wanted to scream, but he couldn't.

Then he heard a voice that rang with an angelic tone. "What is your name?" it said.

"Legion," said the voice he had heard coming from his own lips.

#

Greg Wyatt pulled free from the nurse, and crawled towards the gun. Billy Jackson had collapsed only a foot from the guns, and was now pounding his face into the floor. Blood was pooling beneath him, mixing with saliva that was flying out of his mouth. He looked like a rabid animal, trying to kill anything within sight, including itself.

The State Trooper found his pistol and spun to face the boy. Billy was slowly trying to get to his feet, but he didn't seem to be fully in charge of his limbs. He stood like a child just learning how to walk, and even once he was upright he stumbled and nearly feel. For a moment they locked eyes, and the boy smiled.

Billy Jackson took two forced steps forward.

#

At last Billy could hold on no more. He let go of the bear, and it started to get to its feet. By that time it looked as if his battle no longer mattered. He'd held on long enough to let Greg Wyatt get his gun back.

He was about to die, he knew, but his only regret was that he did not have time to explain everything. Then a gun roared.

In the split second before everything went dark, a flood of memories came flooding back to him. He saw mutilated animals; his dead step-sister; the girls who had died in Louisville before he'd fled to Miltonboro; the bloody bodies of the three girls from Miltonboro; and the very last of all, the dead face of Sarah Clark. That was the thing he saw in the millisecond before the bullet collided with his skull and took all of his worldly problems away.

Epilogue

The headline of the Miltonboro Gazette proclaimed: <u>Murderer Killed</u>. Greg Wyatt stared blankly at the headline as he stood in line at a small gas station, waiting to pay for a cup of coffee. He still hadn't come to grips with what he'd seen in the hospital, but he was going to have some time to do so. He'd been placed on paid administrative leave until his superiors sorted through the whole mess.

Despite the two witnesses in the room, it was still unclear what had happened. The nurse had been in too much of a panic to give a credible story, and her patient didn't even know anything had happened. What it came down to was the report he'd submitted and the evidence. Ultimately the shooting would be ruled righteous, even though Billy Jackson had been unarmed at the time.

Van Miller had escaped unharmed, and was in the process of arranging his release from the hospital. The man still swore that his lifelong patient did not have what took to me a murderer, but everyone knew better than that. They had video footage of the boy choking a gas station clerk with his foot, and he had shot Clem Moss.

The bodies of Rebecca Carol and Sandy Moxley had turned up, as had the body of Sarah Clark. They'd all been killed the exact same way, but Billy had gotten careless by the time he killed them. He'd left fingerprints all over the place, so there hadn't been any doubt that he'd killed them.

The oddest thing was an envelope they'd found at the boy's apartment. It contained a photograph of one of his father's victims, and a handwritten note. A note which had been written by Billy Jackson. Why he'd written, they would never know.

There were some other questions that they would never answer. What had made the young mechanic suddenly turn murderous? Or had he secretly been killing people for years? One day someone might stumble across a basement full of bodies, but they might not. Billy Jackson wouldn't be the first man to start killing people without as much as a sign of trouble.

A young woman with a small toddler was paying for groceries ahead of him, and the child turned and stuck his tongue out. Without even thinking Greg flipped the child off. Then he bit his lip and quickly shoved his hand into his pockets, embarrassed. He'd found himself extremely temperamental since the shooting, but they told him that was to be expected. Officers involved in shootings often showed residual signs.

The little boy he'd flipped off started crying, and clung fearfully to his mother's leg. The woman glanced back at Greg and frowned apologetically. He sighed, relieved that he wouldn't have to try and explain himself.

The woman finished paying and dragged her crying child outside. Greg stepped to the counter with the change for his coffee in hand. He started to pay and leave, then he saw the multi-colored row of candies sitting nearby. He'd never really been a sugar person, but suddenly a bag of peppermints sounded just like the thing he needed.

ABOUT THE AUTHOR

Matthew Alan Hughes lives in western Kentucky with his wife and daughter, and works as a copy editor for the Journal Enterprise Newspaper. He is a graduate of Kentucky Wesleyan College and an alum of Sigma Alpha Mu.

To find out more about his writing, like him on Facebook at "Matthew Alan Hughes, Author".

Acknowledgments

I need to thank several people who have helped me along the way, on The Peppermint Man and other works. First of all is my wonderful wife, Shanda, who has helped me pursue this crazy dream of being a writer. Dr. John Combs, Susan Price and Michael Thomas who proof read the original draft almost a decade ago. Karen Perkins and Bobby Joe Eddings, who taught me the love of writing way back in middle school. Fantasy author Matthew Hughes, I'd stare at our name on the cover of the copy of *Fools Errant* you sent me and just couldn't give up. And lastly fellow author Jeff Ezell, who taught me that its never too late to follow your dreams. Check out Jeff's The Edward Ballister Project.

Also Available from Matthew Alan Hughes....

Short Stories

Mon Couer Mort: My Dead Heart from Post Mortem Press ~2011

The Ghost IS the Machine from Post Mortem Press~2012

Horror Matinee Vol 1 and 2 available for ebook download from the Amazon Kindle Store.

AND COMING FALL OF 2012: *Horror Matinee and other Strange Tales*: **A Collection of Short Fiction by Matthew Alan Hughes**